BEOWULF

BEOWULF

Translated out of the Old English

BY

Chauncey Brewster Tinker, Ph.D.

ASSISTANT PROFESSOR OF ENGLISH IN YALE COLLEGE

REVISED EDITION

NEW YORK
NEWSON & COMPANY
1910

P. W. 1188

TO

FREDERICK BLISS LUQUIENS

PREFACE

THE present translation of *Beowulf* is an attempt to make as simple and readable a version of the poem as is consistent with the character of the original. Archaic forms, which have been much in favor with translators of Old English, have been excluded, because it has been thought that vigor and variety are not incompatible with simple, idiomatic English. The extreme difficulty of choosing an adequate medium has prevented me from attempting a verse-translation. To modern readers, measures imitative of the Old English verse seem quite devoid of rhythm and beauty, while ballad measures and blank verse suggest almost any other period than that of *Beowulf*.

The principal ways in which the present version differs from a merely literal translation are the following: (1) in a rather broad interpretation of pregnant words and phrases; (2) in a conception of some of the Old English compounds as conventional phrases in which the original metaphorical sense is dead; (3) in a free treatment of connecting words; (4) in frequent substitution of a proper name for an ambiguous pronoun.

PREFACE TO THE REVISED EDITION

IN the present edition, foot-notes explanatory of more difficult matters have been added; certain verbal changes introduced in order to bring the text into conformity with improved readings in the original text; and a general attempt made to increase the simplicity and intelligibility of the rendering. In this work, I have been aided by the detailed criticism of Professor F. York Powell, who took a kindly interest in the book from the first. His death has prevented me from making a more satisfactory acknowledgment of his kindness than these ineffectual words.

INTRODUCTORY NOTE

THE Old English poem *Beowulf* is preserved in a single manuscript * in the Cottonian library of the British Museum. Aside from the internal evidences afforded by this manuscript, nothing is known of the origin or authorship of the poem. The handwriting of the manuscript appears to be of the tenth century, but the poem itself is certainly much older. This is evident from the fact that one of the events of the story (the expedition of King Hygelac against the Frisians) is historical, and occurred *ca.* 512. Allowing time for the later events of the story, for the growth of tradition and myth, for the introduction of the Christian coloring, it seems probable that the poem as we now have it is the work of the late seventh century.

All the events of the story take place in Denmark and southern Sweden. England is nowhere mentioned. It is therefore probable that the materials from which the story sprang had been brought together before the last migrations of the

* Cotton Vitellius, A, xv.

Angles to England. However, the poem undoubtedly assumed its final form on English soil. Regarding this gradual growth of the story, there are a number of discrepant views. According to some scholars, the *Beowulf* is of strictly popular origin, like the later English ballads. But the view now generally current is that the poem is the work of one man—an Englishman—who recast the materials brought from the Continent. His work, however, may have been no more than the arrangement and editing of various well-known lays and sagas, and the addition of the Christian elements.

Apart from its literary interest as the oldest of the Germanic epics, the *Beowulf* is invaluable as almost the sole remaining trace of a civilization that preceded the migrations to England.

THE TALE OF BEOWULF

PROLOGUE

Of the Danish kings, they who were ancestors to Hrothgar, and of the passing of Scyld.

Lo! we have learned of the glory of the kings who ruled the Spear-Danes in the olden time, how those princes wrought mighty deeds. Oft did Scyld [1] of the Sheaf wrest the mead-benches from bands of warriors, from many a tribe. The hero bred awe in them from the time when first he was found helpless and outcast; for this he met with comfort, waxed great beneath the sky and throve in honors, until all the neighboring tribes beyond the ocean-paths were brought to serve him and pay him tribute. That was a good king!

In after-time there was born to him in his hall, a young heir whom God sent for a comfort to that people. He saw their sore distress, how in time past [2] they had long suffered for lack of a chief.

[1] That is, "Shield," the defence of his people. He had apparently been found, an outcast babe, adrift in an open boat, with a sheaf of wheat for bed. The term has here become a sort of patronymic.

[2] Before the coming of Scyld.

Therefore, the Lord of life, the King of glory, granted him honor in this world. Beowulf,[1] son of Scyld, was renowned in Danish lands; his fame was spread abroad. So ought a youth to win favor by giving gifts unto his father's friends, that afterwards willing companions may attend him in his age, and the people serve him in time of war.[2] It is by noble deeds that a man shall prosper in any land.

When at length the fated hour was come, Scyld, the valiant, departed unto the keeping of the Lord. Then his dear companions bore him down to the ocean-flood, even as he himself had bidden them, while as yet the friend of the Scyldings ruled them with his words and long did reign over them, dear prince of the land. There at the harbor stood a ship with curving prow, all icy, eager to be gone —meet for a prince. And in the ship's bosom, hard by the mast, they laid that famous hero, their dear lord, the giver of treasure. Many treasures were there, abundance of ornaments brought from afar. Never have I heard men tell of a ship

[1] Not the hero of the poem; nothing else is known of him.

[2] One of the hortatory sentences in which the *Beowulf* abounds. A wise young prince will not neglect to win the favor of his father's *Comitatus* by suitable largess.

more splendidly laden with battle-weapons and
war-harness, with swords and coats of mail. Upon
his breast lay many precious things which were
to go far out with him into the realm of the waters.
Verily no fewer of their gifts and tribal treasures
did this people bestow upon him than they who
at his birth sent him forth alone over the wave,
babe as he was. Moreover, they set up a golden
banner, high above his head, and let the sea bear
him away, giving him over to the deep. Sad at
heart were they, sorrowful in spirit. No man can
truly say—no lord of hall, or hero under heaven
—into whose hands that burden fell.

Part I

BEOWULF AND GRENDEL

I

*Of Hrothgar, son of Healfdene and king of the Scyldings,
and how he built a fair mead-hall, which he named
Heorot. How the merriment in the hall angered
Grendel, an evil monster.*

THEN Beowulf[1] of the Scyldings, dear king
of the nation, was long famous in the cities and
among the peoples—the prince, his father, had
departed from his home[2]—till high Healfdene was
born to him in after-time. He, while he lived,
old and fierce in war, ruled graciously over the
Scyldings. To him there were born into the world
four children after this order: Heorogar, leader of
armies, Hrothgar, and Halga the Good; Queen
Elan, I have heard, was the dear wife of Ongentheow, the brave Scylfing.[3]

[1] Not the hero; compare page 10.   [2] Died.
[3] The rendering of this sentence is extremely uncertain,
owing to the corruption of the MS. Nothing else is known
of the people mentioned.

Then to Hrothgar was given success in battle, glory in warfare, so that his loyal kinsmen gladly obeyed him, until the young warriors were grown, a mighty band. It came into his heart to command his men to build a hall, a mead-hall greater than any that the children of men had ever heard of, and therein to give gifts of all kinds to old and young, as God had prospered him, save the people's land and the lives of men.[1]

And I heard men tell how the work of adorning the people's hall was allotted unto many a tribe, far and wide throughout this earth. After a season—quickly, as man's work prospereth—it came to pass that it was completed for him, this greatest of halls. And he fashioned for it the name of *Heorot*,[2] he whose word had power far and near. He broke not his promise, but gave out rings and treasure at the feast. High and pinnacled, the hall towered aloft. Yet it awaited the surging blaze of hostile fire; nor was it long thereafter that fatal hatred was destined to arise between father-in-law and son-in-law, after the deadly strife.[3]

[1] He respected rights of property and personal liberty.
[2] "Hart"; probably so called from its decoration with antlers.
[3] Epic prophecy; a reference to some tale of the fate of Heorot, familiar to the audience.

Then that mighty spirit[1] who dwelt in darkness bore in his wrath for a season to hear each day the merriment, loud in the hall. There was the sound of the harp, the clear song of the gleeman. He spoke, who could recount from of old the creation of men, told how the Almighty made the earth,[2] the fair-faced land, and the waters that compass it about; how, exultant in victory, He set the sun and moon as lights to lighten the dwellers in the land. He adorned all the regions of the earth with leaf and branch, and created life in everything that lives and moves.

Thus the king's men lived, blissful and happy, until a certain one, a fiend of hell, began to plot mischief. This grim foe was called Grendel, a mighty stalker of the marches, who haunted the moors, the fens and fastnesses. The wretched being had long inhabited the abode of the monster kind, e'er since the Creator had condemned him. The Lord eternal wreaked vengeance upon the kindred of Cain, because of the murder—the slaying of Abel. He got no pleasure in the feud, but for that wicked deed the Lord banished him far from mankind. From him there woke to life all

[1] Grendel.
[2] Cf. *Psalms* 148; *Æneid* 1. 742 ff.

14

evil broods—monsters and elves and sea-beasts,
and giants too, who long time strove with God.
He gave them their reward.

II

Grendel falls upon Heorot and slays thirty heroes. Hrothgar
and his men are helpless before the monster, and the
destruction is continued for twelve winters.

As soon as night was come, he set out for the
high-built hall, to see how the Ring-Danes were
faring after the drinking of the mead. And he
found therein a band of warrior-nobles sleeping
after feast. They knew naught of sorrow, that
wretched lot of all mankind. The creature of
destruction, fierce and greedy, wild and furious,
was ready straight. He seized thirty thanes upon
their bed. Then back he returned to his abode,
exulting in his booty, back to his lair with his
fill of slaughter.

Then at dawn, with break of day, Grendel's
deeds were manifest to men, and the voice of
weeping was uplifted—a great cry at morn, after
their feast. The great lord, the prince exceeding
good, sat joyless, when they had looked upon the

15

track of the monster, the accursèd foe; the mighty hero suffered, sorrowing for his thanes. Too great was that strife, too loathsome and lasting.

It was no longer than a single night ere he wrought more deeds of murder; he recked not of the feud and the crime—he was too fixed in them. Then, when the hatred of that thane of hell was fully known to them, truly told by tokens manifest, it was easy to find the man who sought him out a resting-place elsewhere more at large, a bed among the bowers of the hall. He kept himself thereafter further aloof and more secure, whosoever escaped the fiend.

Thus he held sway, and alone against them all fought accursedly, until that best of houses stood empty. Long was the time: for twelve winters the friend of the Scyldings suffered distress, yea, every woe, uttermost sorrow. And so it became known to the children of men—sadly told in song —that Grendel had long been fighting against Hrothgar, and for many a season had waged a bitter war and wicked feud, an unending strife. He would not stay the waste of life out of compassion toward any of the Danish race, compounding with them for tribute, and none of the wise men could look for a fair ransom from the destroyer's hands. The dread monster, like a dark shadow of death, kept pursuing warrior and youth; he trapped and ensnared them. Night after night he haunted the misty moors. Men know not whither hell's sorcerers wander in their rounds.

Thus the enemy of man, the terrible lone wanderer, oft wrought many a foul deed, much grievous affliction. In the dark of the night-tide he took up his abode in Heorot, the hall brightly adorned. Hrothgar could not approach the throne, precious in the sight of God, nor did he know His love.[1]

Mighty grief and heart-break was this for the kind lord of the Scyldings to bear. Many mighty men oft sat in council and deliberated together touching what it were best for great-hearted men to do against these sudden terrors. Sometimes they vowed sacrifices at their idol-fanes; the people prayed aloud that the Destroying Spirit [2] would aid them in the torment that had fallen upon them. Such was their custom,[3] such their heathen faith;

[1] The subject of this sentence, not plainly indicated in the original, may perhaps be Grendel. One spot was inviolate. But no thoroughly satisfactory explanation has ever been given.

[2] The devil.

[3] The rest of the section is usually regarded as the interpolation of a Christian scribe.

the thoughts of their heart were turned on hell; they knew not the Creator, Judge of deeds; they wist not of the Lord God; verily, they knew naught of the worship of the Ruler of heaven, the King of glory.

Woe unto him who through deadly hate [1] is doomed to thrust his soul into the fiery abyss, to hope for no comfort, no change in anywise. But blessed is the man who at his death may go unto the Lord and find refuge in the Father's bosom.

III

In the far country of the Geats, Beowulf hears of Grendel's deeds, and resolves to go to the help of Hrothgar. He makes him ready a great ship and sails with his men to the country of the Danes. On landing he is accosted by the shore-guard.

So the son of Healfdene [2] kept ever brooding over his sorrow. The wise hero could not stay the suffering; too grievous, too long and heart-sickening, was the struggle which had come upon that people, a cruel plague, greatest of evils that walk by night.

---

[1] The notion is not clear; hatred of the new Christianity, perhaps.   [2] Hrothgar.

A thane of Hygelac,[1] great among the Geats, heard of these deeds of Grendel in his native land. In his strength he was the best of men in the day of this life, noble and mighty. He bade make ready for him a goodly ship, saying that he would go over the ocean-road unto that war-king, the great prince, since he had need of men. Little did his prudent thanes blame him for that journey, though he was dear to them; they encouraged him in his high purpose, and looked for good omens. The hero had warriors, chosen from among the Geats, the keenest he could find. Fifteen in all went down unto the ship. A skilled mariner pointed out the landmarks unto them.

Time wore on. The ship was upon the waves, the boat under the cliff. The ready warriors mounted the prow. The ocean-streams dashed the waves upon the beach. The men bore rich armor into the bosom of the ship, splendid war-harness. The warriors pushed off their tight-fitted craft on the willing adventure. So, driven by the wind, the bark most like unto a bird, sped foamy-necked across the waves, until, about the same hour the second day, the curving prow had jour-

[1] Beowulf, hero of the poem.

neyed on so far that the sailors caught sight of
land, saw gleaming cliffs and lofty hills, broad
ocean-headlands. Thus the sea was crossed, and
the voyage ended. Then the Weder people [1] went
quickly up ashore, and made fast their ship, while
their mail-coats and battle-raiment clashed. And
they thanked God that their sea-paths had been
easy.

The guard of the Scyldings, he who had been
set to watch the headland, saw them from the
cliff, bearing over the gangway their bright shields
and ready weapons. His heart was spurred with
longing to know who the men were. So the thane
of Hrothgar went down to the shore, riding upon
his horse. He shook his spear mightily with his
hands, and asked in fitting words: "What warriors
are ye, in coats of mail, who come hither, sailing
your great ship over the sea, the ocean-paths? I
have been warden of the coast and have kept
watch by the sea that no foe with force of ships
might do harm in the Danish land. No shield-
bearers have ever tried more openly to land here,
nor did ye know at all the password, the agree-
ment of the warriors, our kinsmen. Never have
I seen a mightier hero upon earth, a mightier man

[1] Another name for the Geats.

20

in armor, than is one of you. He is no common
thane decked out with weapons, unless his face,
his matchless countenance, belie him. But now
I must know your lineage from you, ye false spies,
ere ye go further in the land of the Danes. Now
ye seafarers, strangers from afar, give ear to my
plain counsel: it were best to make known forthwith whence ye are come."

IV

*Beowulf makes answer touching the purpose of his coming,
and is guided by the coast-warden to Heorot.*

THE chieftain, leader of the band, answered
him again and unlocked the treasure of his speech:
"We are men of the Geatish kin, and Hygelac's
hearth-companions. My father was well known
among the peoples, a noble prince named Ecgtheow.[1] He lived many winters ere, full of years,
he went his way from home. Him well nigh every
wise man remembers, the wide world over. With
friendly purpose we are come to thy lord, the son
of Healfdene, guardian of the people. Give us thy
gracious counsel; we have a great errand to the

[1] Nothing further is known of the events here touched
upon.

21

mighty lord of the Danes. Naught secret shall there be in that which I intend. Thou knowest if it be, as we have heard for a truth, that some foe among the Scyldings, a secret destroyer, causes on dark nights by the terror of his coming unutterable evil, shame and slaughter. Now by my great mind I may perchance give counsel to Hrothgar, how he, the wise and good, can overcome the foe; if this burden of anguish be destined ever to leave him, release come once again, and the waves of care wax cooler; or else, ever after, shall he suffer seasons of affliction, wretched misery, long as the noblest of houses stands there in its lofty place."

The warden spoke, the fearless servant, there where he sat upon his horse: "A keen shield-warrior, he who judges well, must know the difference between words and deeds. I learn that this is a band friendly to the lord of the Scyldings. Go forth, then, with your weapons and your armor. I will guide you. Likewise, I will command the thanes, my kinsmen, to guard your ship with honor against every foe, the new-tarred boat there upon the strand, until the bark with curving prow bear the dear master back over the ocean-streams to Wedermark. Unto so brave a man be it granted to endure unharmed the shock of conflict."

Then they departed along their way; the boat
lay quiet, the broad-bosomed ship rested on her
moorings, fast at anchor. The boar-images above
their golden cheek-guards glistened[1]; bright were
they, and hardened in the fire—there the boar kept
guard. The men hurried on in warlike mood;
they hastened, marching on together, till they
caught sight of the well-built hall, stately and
bright with gold. It was the greatest among the
dwellings of men beneath the skies; in it dwelt the
king, and its light shone over many lands. Then
the bold chief[2] pointed out to them that radiant
dwelling of brave men that they might straightway
go to it. He—himself a warrior—turned his horse
and spoke a word to them: "It is time for me to
go. May the Almighty Father by his grace keep
you safe in your adventures. I will down to the
sea to keep watch against hostile bands."

[1] Carven figures worn as charms upon the helmet.
[2] The coast-guard.

V

Beowulf and his men come to Heorot. They are met by the herald, who tells their coming to King Hrothgar.

THE street was brightly set with stones;[1] this path guided the band of men. The byrnie gleamed, hard and hand-locked, the bright iron rings sang in the armor, as they came marching to the hall in battle-harness. Weary of the sea, they placed their shields, bucklers wondrous hard, against the wall of the house; they sat down upon the benches.[2] Their byrnies rang, harness of heroes. Their ashen spears stood together, gray-shafted weapons of the seamen. This armored band was well adorned with weapons.

Then a proud warrior asked the heroes concerning their lineage: "Whence bring ye your plated shields, your gray war-shirts, and your visored helmets and this group of spears? I am Hrothgar's servant and herald. Never have I seen so great a band of strangers of more courageous mood. I think that ye have sought out Hrothgar

[1] Notice the poet's interest in a paved road.
[2] Outside the hall.

nowise as exiles, but from valor and out of the greatness of your hearts."

And the proud lord of the Weder people, famed for his strength, answered him again; he spoke a word to him, bold under his helmet: "We are table-companions of Hygelac. Beowulf is my name. I will tell my errand to the son of Healfdene, the great king thy lord, if he will grant us to draw nigh to him who is so good."

Wulfgar spoke (he was a chief of the Wendels, his boldness was known to many, his wisdom and might): "I will ask the friend of the Danes, king of the Scyldings, giver of rings, the mighty lord, touching thy journey, as thou dost entreat, and will straightway make known to thee what answer the good king thinketh meet to give me."

And he went quickly to where Hrothgar was sitting, old and exceeding white-haired, with his company of thanes; the valiant man went until he stood before the face of the lord of the Danes— he knew the custom of the court. Wulfgar spoke to his friendly lord: "Hither are come across the sea-waves travelers, Geatish men from a far coun- try. Warriors call their chieftain Beowulf. They beg to have speech with thee, my lord. Re- fuse not to converse with them, O gracious Hrothgar. In their equipment they seem worthy of the esteem of heroes, and verily the chief who led the warriors hither is a man of valor."

VI

Beowulf is graciously welcomed by the king, and thereupon tells how he will fight with Grendel.

THEN spoke Hrothgar, defence of the Scyldings: "I knew him when he was a child; his aged father was called Ecgtheow, to whom at his home Hrethel the Geat gave his only daughter in marriage. His bold son is now come hither to a loyal friend. Moreover, seafarers, who carried thither rich gifts as good-will offerings to the Geats, have said that he, strong in battle, had in the grip of his hand the strength of thirty men. Him holy God hath sent us, as I hope, to be a gracious help to the West-Danes against the terror of Grendel. I shall proffer the hero gifts for his boldness Make haste and bid all the band of kinsmen come in together unto us. Say to them, moreover, that they are welcome among the Danish people."

Then Wulfgar came to the door of the hall and announced the word from within: "My victorious lord, prince of the East-Danes, bids me say that he knows your noble lineage, and that ye, as men of stout courage, are welcome unto him hither over the billows of the sea. Now ye may go in unto Hrothgar in your war-array, under your helmets; but let your spears, shafts of slaughter, here await the issue of your words."

Then the mighty one arose with many a warrior round him—it was a noble group of thanes. Some remained and guarded the armor as the chief bade them. The heroes hastened, as the guide led them under the roof of Heorot. The great-hearted man, bold under his helmet, went on until he stood within the hall. Beowulf spoke—on him gleamed his byrnie, his coat of mail linked by the smith's craft—: "Hail to thee, Hrothgar! I am Hygelac's kinsman and thane. Many an exploit have I undertaken in the days of my youth. In my native land I learned of Grendel's deeds; for sea-farers say that this hall, this best of houses, stands empty and useless for all men, as soon as evening light is hidden under the vault of heaven. And my people, even the best and wisest men among them, urged me, king Hrothgar, to come to thee, for they knew the strength of my might. They had themselves beheld when I came from the fight, stained with the blood of my foes. There had I bound five of my enemies, destroyed a giant race, and slain by night the sea-beasts on the wave.[1] I endured great distress, avenged the affliction of the Weder people—they who had suffered woes. I ground the angry foe in pieces. And now I alone will decide the fight with Grendel, the giant monster. One boon I beg of thee, prince of the Bright Danes, defence of the Scyldings:—Deny me not, thou shield of warriors, friend of the people, now I am come so far, that I alone, I and my band of thanes, this my brave company, may cleanse Heorot of the evil that has come upon it. I have learned, too, that the monster in his rashness recks not of weapons. Therefore, that the heart of Hygelac my lord may be gladdened because of me, I scorn to carry sword or broad shield, the yellow buckler, into the fight; but with my hands I will grapple the fiend and fight for life, foe against foe. He whom death taketh must rely upon the judgment of the Lord. I think that if he can prevail in the hall of war he will fearlessly devour the Geats even as he has often devoured the best of the Hrethmen.[2] Thou shalt have no need to bury my head if death take me,

[1] Cf. the tale on page 34.   [2] Danes.

for he will have me, all red with gore; he will bear
away the corpse to feast upon it; the lone wanderer will pitilessly eat it, staining his moor-haunts;
thou needst not then take more thought for the
sustenance of my body. But send thou to Hygelac, if the fight take me, the matchless mail, best
of armors, that guards my breast; it is a relic of
Hrethel,[1] and the work of Weland.[2] Wyrd[3] ever
goeth her destined course."

VII

*Hrothgar makes answer touching the deeds of Grendel.
   They feast in Heorot.*

THEN spoke Hrothgar, defence of the Scyldings: "With kindly help, my friend Beowulf, thou
hast come to fight in our defence. Thy father
fought the greatest of feuds, for he slew with his
hand Heatholaf among the Wylfings; wherefore
the Weder people, in dread of war, could not harbor him.[4] From there he fled over the rolling

[1] His grandfather, once king of the Geats.
[2] The mythical smith of English and Norse legend.
Cf. *Deor's Lament.*
[3] The Germanic goddess of Fate.
[4] He had forfeited his tribal rights by the murder of
Heatholaf. Nothing further is known of the incident.

waves to the South-Danes, the honored Scyldings;
at the time when I first ruled the Danish folk, and
in my youth held the wealthy city of heroes, rich
in treasure, for Heorogar, Healfdene's son, was
dead, my elder brother lifeless;—he was a better
man than I. Afterwards I se tled that feud with
money; I sent olden treasures [1] to the Wylfings
across the ocean's back; and Ecgtheow swore oaths
to me.[2]

"Sorrowful am I in soul to tell to any man what
shame and sudden mischief Grendel has wrought
for me in Heorot out of his hateful thoughts. My
hall-troop,[3] my warrior-band, is melted away.
Wyrd hath swept them away into the horrid clutch
of Grendel. God alone can easily check the deeds
of that mad foe. Full oft my warriors, after the
drinking of the beer, have boastfully vowed over
their ale-cups to await with their dread swords the
onset of Grendel in the hall. Then in the morning, when shone the day, this mead-hall, this
lordly house, was all stained with blood, the
benches reeking with gore—the hall was drenched
in blood. So, the fewer loyal men, beloved war-

[1] Weregild for Heatholaf.
[2] To serve him, or to keep the peace.
[3] Comitatus. For the whole subject of this important
institution, see Tacitus, *Germania* 13-14.

riors, had I then because of those whom death did snatch away. Sit now to the feast, and unseal to men as thy mind moveth thee, the thoughts of thy heart, and all thy confidence of victory."

Then in the mead-hall a bench was made ready for the Geatmen, one and all. Thither the stout-hearted men went to sit in the pride of their strength. A thane did service, who bore a chased ale-flagon in his hand, and poured out the bright mead. At times a bard sang, clear-voiced in Heorot. There was merriment among the heroes, no little company of Danes and Weders.

VIII AND IX

Unferth, a thane of Hrothgar, grows jealous of Beowulf and taunts him, raking up old tales of a swimming-match with Breca. Beowulf is angered and boastfully tells the truth touching that adventure, and puts Unferth to silence. Queen Wealhtheow passes the cup. Hrothgar commends Heorot to the care of Beowulf.

UNFERTH, the son of Ecglaf, who sat at the feet of the lord of the Scyldings, spoke, and stirred up a quarrel; the coming of Beowulf, the brave seafarer, vexed him sore, for he would not that any other man under heaven should ever win more glories in this world than he himself. "Art thou that Beowulf who didst strive with Breca on the broad sea and didst contend with him in swimming, when ye two, foolhardy, made trial of the waves and for a mad boast risked your lives in the deep water? None, friend or foe, could turn you from the sorry venture when ye two swam out upon the sea. But ye enfolded the ocean-streams with your arms, measured the sea-streets, buffeted the water with your hands, gliding over the deep. The ocean was tossing with waves, a winter's sea. Seven nights ye toiled in the power of the waters; and he overcame thee in the match, for he had the greater strength. Then at morning-tide the sea cast him up on the coast of the Heathoræmas, whence he, beloved of his people, went to his dear fatherland, the country of the Brondings, and his own fair city where he was lord of a stronghold, and of subjects and treasure. Verily the son of Beanstan made good all his boast against thee. Wherefore, though thou hast ever been valiant in the rush of battle, I look to a grim fight, yea, and a worse issue, for thee, if thou darest for the space of one night abide near Grendel."

Beowulf, son of Ecgtheow, spoke: "Well! thou hast said a deal about Breca in thy drunkenness, Unferth my friend, and hast talked much of his adventure. The truth now I tell, that I had more sea strength, more battling with the waves, than any man else. We talked of this when boys, and boasted, being yet in the days of our youth, that we would venture our lives out at sea; and we performed it even so. Naked in our hands, we held our hard swords as we swam, purposing to defend us against the whales. He, nowise swifter on the flood, could not swim far from me through the waves, nor would I part from him. Thus we two were in the sea for the space of five nights,[1] till the flood, the tossing waves, coldest of weathers, and darkening night drove us apart, and a fierce north wind beat down upon us;—rough were the waves. The wrath of the sea-fish was roused; then my shirt of mail, hard and hand-wrought, was of help to me against the foes; my woven armor, gold-adorned, lay upon my breast. An evil monster dragged me to the bottom; the grim foe held me fast in its clutch; yet it was granted me to strike the creature with the point of my war-sword; the

[1] Is this to be understood as a correction of Unferth's extravagance in saying seven?

fierce struggle carried off the mighty sea-beast by my hand.[1]

"Thus did the evil creatures often press me hard, but as was meet, I served them well with my war-sword; they had no joyous fill, by eating me, wicked destroyers, sitting round their feast nigh the bottom of the sea; but on the morrow, wounded by my sword, slain by the dagger, they lay up along the sea-strand so that they could nevermore hinder seafarers on their course in the deep channel.

"Light came from the east, the bright beacon of the Lord; the waves were stilled, and I could descry the sea-headlands, those wind-swept walls. Wyrd often saveth the warrior not doomed to die, if he be of good courage. Howbeit, it was granted me to slay nine sea-beasts with the sword. Never yet have I heard of a more desperate nightly struggle under the vault of heaven, nor of a man more sore beset in ocean-streams; yet I escaped with my life from the clutch of my foes, though spent with my adventure. The sea, the current of the flood, bore me on to the land of the Finns.

"Naught have I heard of like exploits on thy

[1] This fight should be compared with the encounter with Grendel's mother, pages 75 ff.

part, naught of the terror of thy sword. Breca
never yet, nay, nor either of you, hath wrought
so boldly in the play of battle with blood-stained
swords—I boast not much of that—though thou
wast the slayer of thine own brethren, thy next
of kin; for that thou shalt be damned in hell,
good though thy wit may be. I say to thee truly,
thou son of Ecglaf, that Grendel, the fell monster,
had never wrought against thy lord so many awful
deeds, this shame in Heorot, were thy mind and
heart so fierce in battle as thou thyself sayest.
But he has found that he need not greatly fear
the enmity, the dread attack, of thy people, the
Victor-Scyldings. He takes forced tribute from
you; he spares none of the Danish people, but he
preys at will upon you; he kills and feasts,
and looks not for resistance from the Spear-
Danes. I, however, will show him ere long the
strength and courage of the Geats in fight. Thereafter let him who may, go proudly to the mead-
drinking when the morning-light of another day,
the sun in its radiance, shines from the south over
the children of men."

Then rejoiced the giver of treasure, the gray-
haired king, famous in battle; the prince of
the Bright-Danes trusted in him for help; the

shepherd of the people heard from Beowulf his
firm resolve. And the laughter[1] of the thanes
arose; loud rang the din and joyous were their
words.

Wealhtheow, Hrothgar's queen, went forth,
mindful of courtesies; in her gold array she greeted
the men in the hall. The noble lady first gave the
cup to him who guarded the land of the East-Danes;
she bade him, beloved of his people, be blithe at
the beer-drinking. The victorious [2] king partook
in gladness of the feast and the hall-cup. Then
the lady of the Helmings moved about to old and
young in every part of the hall, handing the costly
cup, until the moment came when the diademed
queen, noble of mind, bore the cup to Beowulf.
She greeted the lord of the Geats, and thanked
God, discreet in her words, that the desire of her
heart was brought to pass, that she might put her
trust in some hero for relief from all her affliction.
That warrior, fierce in strife, received the cup
from Wealhtheow; and then, eager for the fight,
Beowulf, son of Ecgtheow, spoke and said: "I
made this vow when I put to sea and embarked
with my band of men; that I would either wholly

[1] Perhaps at the discomfiture of Unferth.
[2] The epithet, as often, is purely formal.

fulfil the desire of your people, or fall in struggle,
fast in the grip of the fiend. I will bravely accom-
plish noble deeds or abide mine end in this mead-
hall." These words, these boastings of the Geat,
were well-pleasing to the lady; the noble queen, in
her array of gold, went to sit by her lord.

Then again as of old [1] the great word was spoken
in that hall; joyous was the company—there was
the sound of a mighty people—until of a sudden
the son of Healfdene was minded to go to his evening rest; for he knew that the monster intended
war upon the high hall (as soon as men could no
more see the light of the sun, and shadowy creatures came gliding forth, wan beneath the clouds,
night darkening over all.[2]) The whole company
arose. Hrothgar greeted Beowulf—hero greeted
hero—and wished him well, wished him the mas-
tery in the wine-hall, and spoke this word: "Never,
since I could lift hand and shield, have I entrusted
unto any man this royal hall of the Danes, save now
to thee. Have thou and hold this best of houses;
bethink thee of thy mighty deeds, show forth thy
valiant strength, be watchful against the foe. Thy

[1] Before the coming of Grendel; or perhaps, before
Wealhtheow's entry.
[2] Cf. *Macbeth* 3. 2, l. 50.

desires shall not be unsatisfied, if thou escape with
thy life from the great adventure."

X

*They leave Beowulf and his men alone in the hall. Grendel
draws nigh.*

AND Hrothgar, lord of the Scyldings, went out
of the hall with his company of men; for the war-
rior-chief was minded to go unto Wealhtheow, his
queen and consort. The glorious king,[1] as men
have learned, had set a guardian in the hall to wait
for Grendel; Beowulf did special service for the
lord of the Danes, keeping watch against the coming of the monster. Verily, the chief of the Geats
trusted surely in his mighty strength and in the
favor of the Lord. Then he put off his iron byrnie
and took the helmet from his head; his jeweled
sword, choicest of weapons, he gave to his thane,
bidding him take charge of his war-armor. Then,
ere he mounted upon his bed, Beowulf, the great
Geat, spoke a boastful word: "I deem myself nowise lesser than Grendel in my deeds of warfare;
therefore, not with the sword will I quell him and
take his life, though I am fully able. He knows

---

[1] Perhaps meaning God.

not the use of good weapons—how to strike at me,
and hew my shield—famed though he be in evil
deeds; but we two this night will forego the sword
if he dare come to the fight without a weapon.
Thereafter let all-knowing God, the holy Lord,
adjudge the victory to whichsoever it be, as seemeth meet to Him."

Then the brave warrior laid him down and the
pillow received the face of the hero, and round
about him many a bold seaman sank down upon
his bed. None of them thought ever again to reach
the home he loved, his kinsfolk, or the town where
he was bred; for they had heard that a bloody death
had already destroyed far too many of the Danish
men in that wine-hall. But the Lord wove victory
for them, granting unto the Weder [1] people comfort and help, inasmuch as they were all to overcome their foe by one man's might and by his
single strength. And thus the truth is manifest
that Almighty God hath ruled mankind throughout
all time.

In the gloom of the night came stalking that
ranger of the dark. The watchmen [1] slept, they
who had been set to guard the horn-gabled hall—
all slept, save one—for it was well known to men

[1] The Geats.

39

that the ruthless destroyer could not drag them beneath the shades when the Creator willed it not.
But Beowulf, wrathfully watching for the foe,
awaited in anger the issue of the fight.

XI

*Grendel comes into Heorot and devours one of the men.
Beowulf grapples the monster.*

THEN from the moorland, beneath the misty hill-
sides, came Grendel drawing near; and God's
wrath was on him. The deadly foe was thinking
to ensnare some man in that high hall. On he
strode beneath the clouds, until he could see full
well the wine-hall, the gilded house of men, all
bright with gold. This was not the first time that
he had sought out Hrothgar's home, but never in
all the days of his life, before or since, did he
meet among hall-thanes, warriors more sturdy.
So the creature, of all joys bereft, came roaming
on unto the hall. The door, though fast in fire-
hardened bands, sprang open straightway, soon
as he touched it with his hands.[1] Thus, plotting
evil, he burst open the entrance to the hall, for he

---

[1] An evidence of Grendel's magic power. The incident
seems to be imitated in the *Legend of St. Andrew*, l. 1001.

was swollen with rage. Quickly thereafter the
fiend was treading the bright-paved floor, moving
on in wrathful mood. Out of his eyes started a
loathsome light, most like to flame. He saw in
the hall many warriors, a kindred band together, a
group of clansmen all asleep. And he laughed in
his heart. The cursèd monster thought to take
the life from each body, ere the day broke; for the
hope of a plenteous feast was come to him. But
he was not fated to devour any more of the race
of men after that night.

The mighty kinsman of Hygelac was watching
to see how the deadly foe would go about his swift
attacks. The monster thought not of tarrying,
but on a sudden, for his first move, he seized upon
a sleeping thane, rent him in pieces unawares, bit
into the flesh, drank the blood from the veins, and
swallowed him in huge pieces. In a moment he
had devoured the whole corpse, even the hands
and feet. He stepped on nearer and seized with
his hands the great-hearted warrior on his bed.
The fiend clutched at him with his claw, but Beowulf quickly grasped it with deadly purpose, fas-
tening upon the arm. Straightway that master of
evils discovered that never in this world in all the
corners of the earth, had he met in any man a might-

41

ier hand-grip. He was troubled in heart and soul; but he could get away never the faster for that. He was eager to be off; he wished to flee away into the darkness, to rejoin the horde of devils. He was not faring there as in former days. Then the good kinsman of Hygelac bethought him of his speech at even[1]; he stood upright and grappled him fast; his fingers burst and bled.[2] The giant was making off. The hero followed close. The monster was minded to fling loose, if he could, and flee away thence to the fen-hollows; but he knew that the strength of his arm was in the grasp of an angry foe. A dire journey had the destroyer made to Heorot.

Loud rang the lordly hall. All the Danes dwelling in that city, nobles and heroes every one, were struck with terror. Furious were both the maddened wrestlers. The house reëchoed. It was a great wonder that the wine-hall withstood these battling foemen, that the fair building fell not to the ground; save that all within and without it was so firmly strengthened by iron bands, cunningly forged. There, as I have heard men tell, many a

[1] See pages 35 ff.
[2] Grendel's fingers burst as a result of Beowulf's grip. Cf. *Nibelungenlied* B 675.

42

mead-bench, gold-adorned, started from its base,
where the fierce ones were struggling.   The wise
councilors of the Scyldings had thought that none
among men would ever be able to wreck by force
this goodly house, bedecked with bones, nor to
destroy it by craft, unless perchance the fire's embrace should swallow it in smoke.[1]

A noise arose, oft renewed; a ghastly terror fell
on all the North-Danes who heard the shrieking in
the house, heard God's enemy yelling out his horrid song, chant of the vanquished—Hell's captive
howling o'er his wound.   He held him fast who in
his strength was the mightiest of men in the day of
this life.

XII

Beowulf has the victory, and tears out Grendel's arm.   The
monster escapes to the fen with his death-wound.

THE defence of heroes would by no means let
the murderer escape alive—he counted his life of
no avail to any of the people.   There many a warrior of Beowulf's drew his old sword; they thought
to protect the life of their lord, the great prince, if
so they might.   They knew not, those brave war-

[1] A hint of the subsequent fate of Heorot; see page 13.

riors, when they plunged into the fight, thinking to hack the monster on every side and take his life, that not the choicest blade on earth nor battle-axe could graze that foul destroyer; for he had bound by a spell weapons of war and every edged sword. Yet he was doomed to die a wretched death in the day of this life; the outcast spirit must needs journey far away into the power of fiends. There found that foe to God, who oft ere now in mirthful mood had wrought mischief for the children of men, that his wound-proof body availed him not, for the valiant kinsman of Hygelac had got him by the hand. Hateful to each was the life of the other. The evil beast endured sore pain of body. Upon his shoulder a gaping wound appeared; the sinews sprang asunder, the flesh was rent apart. The glory of the fight was given to Beowulf. Grendel, sick to death, was doomed to flee thence and find out his joyless abode beneath the fen-banks. Full well he knew that the end of his life was come, the appointed number of his days. By that deadly fight the desire of all the Danes was satisfied.

Thus he who came from far, wise and valiant in spirit, had cleansed Hrothgar's hall and freed it from danger. He rejoiced in the night's work, in his heroic deeds.   The lord of the Geats had made good his boast to the East-Danes, for he had saved them out of all their affliction, the harrowing torment, no little sorrow, which they had suffered and were doomed to bear in sad necessity.   A token of the fight was seen, when, beneath the spacious roof, the warrior flung down the hand and arm and shoulder—the whole limb and claw of Grendel.

XIII

The Danes rejoice.   They go and look upon the mere whither Grendel escaped, and return to Heorot, racing their horses and listening to the tale of the bard.

In the morning, as I have heard, many warriors were about the gift-hall; chieftains came from far and near to gaze upon the wonder, the traces of the foe.   Grievous seemed his death to none of those who beheld the tracks of the inglorious one; how he, weary at heart, vanquished in strife, doomed and hunted, took his last steps to the Nicors' [1] mere. There the waters were seething with blood, the awful surge of the waves welled up, all mingled with blood and hot gore.   Death-doomed he discolored all the flood, when, in his joyless lair, he

[1] Sea-beasts'.

laid down his life, his heathen soul; there Hell got him.

Thence returned the thanes and many a youth from their glad journey, proudly riding from the mere upon their horses, heroes upon white steeds. There was proclaimed the greatness of Beowulf. Full oft 'twas said that south or north, between the seas, o'er all the broad earth beneath the arch of heaven, none among shield-bearing warriors was of higher worth, none more worthy of kingdom. They did not in the least say aught against their own kind lord, gracious Hrothgar, for he was a good king.

At times the warriors made their yellow steeds gallop or run a race, where the ways seemed good to them and known for their excellence.

At times one of the king's thanes, whose memory was full of songs,[1] laden with vaunting rimes, who knew old tales without number, invented a new story, a truthful tale; the man deftly narrated the adventure of Beowulf, and cunningly composed other skilful lays with interwoven words.

[1] Songs boasting of personal prowess, or of the might of national heroes.

THE LAY OF SIGEMUND

*The bard sings how Sigemund, the Volsung, slew a mighty
  dragon; and how Heremod, a Danish king, was a sore
  burden to his people, much unlike Beowulf.*

He told everything that he had heard of the mighty
exploits of Sigemund, much that had ne'er been told:—
the battle-toil of the Wælsing,[1] distant journeyings, feuds
and crimes, of which the children of men knew nothing,
save Fitela,[2] the nephew who was with his uncle when he
would repeat aught touching these things; for they were
comrades at need in every strife. They had slain with
their swords many of the monster broods. Sigemund,
after his death, attained no little glory, since, brave in
battle, he had slain the dragon who kept guard over the
treasure. Alone beneath the gray rock, the prince ventured
the daring deed, nor was Fitela with him. Nevertheless,
it was granted unto him that his sword, the noble iron,
pierced the wondrous serpent and stood fast in the wall.
The dragon died the death. The dread warrior had won
by his valor the enjoyment of the treasure, all at his own
will. The son of Wæls[3] loaded his sea-boat and bore the
glittering treasures into the bosom of his ship. Heat
consumed the serpent. In his daring exploits he was by
far the most famed of adventurers among the nations,

[1] Volsung. See the Norse saga. This is one of the
earliest extant references to the Volsung myth, centuries
older than the Norse saga and the German poem.
[2] Sinfiötli, his sister's son.
[3] Volsung, Sigemund.

47

this defence of warriors; wherefore he throve in days gone by.

After Heremod's[1] war-strength waned, his power and might, he was betrayed into the hands of his enemies, the Eotens,[2] and sent speedily away. Overwhelming sorrows disabled him too long; he became a lifelong care to his people, to all his nobles. Oft had the hero's life been bewailed in former days by many a prudent man, who had trusted his lord for protection from harm—trusted that the prince would prosper, attain his father's lordship, guard the nation, the treasure and sheltering city, the realm of heroes, fatherland of the Scyldings. Beowulf, the kinsman of Hygelac, was more gracious to all the children of men and to his friends. Sorrow befell Heremod.

At times, in races with their steeds, they measured the yellow roads. And the morning-light was thrust forth and urged onwards.[3] Many a stout-hearted warrior went to the high hall to see the great wonder. Likewise, the king himself, guardian of the treasure, famed for his virtues, walked forth in glory from the bower with a great company; and his queen with him, amidst a bevy

[1] This incident, so awkwardly introduced, is probably intended to contrast the craven with the hero. Sigemund is compared, Heremod contrasted, with Beowulf. Heremod was an old king of the Danes—Scyld's predecessor possibly.

[2] Finns.

[3] The metaphorical expression may be derived from the launching of a boat. Day advanced.

48

of maidens, passed up the path to the mead-hall.

XIV

Hrothgar and his men look upon Grendel's arm in Heorot. The king and Beowulf speak touching the fight.

HROTHGAR spoke:—he went to the hall, stood in the entrance, gazed on the high roof bright with gold, and on the arm of Grendel: "Now for this sight be thanks to God straightway! Much evil, many hardships, have I endured at the hands of Grendel; but God, the King of glory, can evermore work wonder upon wonder. It was but now that I thought never to be delivered from any of my woe, while this best of houses stood drenched with blood and gore. The affliction scattered all my wise men, who thought that they could nevermore defend this stronghold of the people from hated foes, from demons and devils. Now, through the might of the Lord, a man hath wrought a deed which all of us erewhile with our craft were unable to compass. Lo! the woman, whoe'er she be, that gave birth to this son among the tribes of men may say, if she be yet alive, that our God of old hath been gracious unto her in child-bearing.

"Now, O Beowulf, thou best of men, I will love thee like a son within my heart. Hold fast henceforth this our new-made kinship. Thou shalt not lack any good thing of earth within my power. Full oft for lesser deeds have I given rich gifts of honor unto a meaner warrior, a weaker in the fight. By thy deeds thou hast attained that thy glory liveth for ever and ever. May the Almighty ever reward thee as now He hath."

Then spoke Beowulf, son of Ecgtheow: "Fighting with great good-will, we wrought that mighty deed; boldly we met the power of the unknown. But I would indeed that thou couldst have seen the creature himself in full gear, the fiend wearied nigh to fainting. Grappling him there, I thought to fix him fast on his death-bed so that he should lie struggling for life in my grip, unless his body vanished utterly away.[1] But I could not stop his going, for the Lord willed it not. I did not cleave well unto the mortal foe, for the fiend was too powerful upon his feet. Yet, in saving his life, he left his claw behind, his arm and shoulder, to mark his track. But the wretched creature has not bought him any solace thus; none the longer will the evil-doer live, weighed down by sin. But pain has

[1] By virtue of his magic power.

got him close in its deadly clasp, within its baleful
bonds.   There, stained with sin, shall he abide the
Great Doom—how the glorious Judge shall assign
him his portion."

Then, in his boastful speech, that son of Ecglaf [1]
kept more silent touching warlike deeds, after all
the nobles had beheld the arm before them, there
upon the lofty roof, the fiendish claw, won by the
hero's might.   Most like to steel were all the nails,
the hand-spurs, horrible spikes of the heathen foe.
All declared that no warrior's sword, albeit keen,
could have grazed the monster so as to strike off
that bloody talon.

XV

*They adorn Heorot for the feast.   Hrothgar bestows gifts
upon Beowulf.*

Straightway it was bidden that Heorot be
adorned within by the hand of man.   Many men
there were and women to prepare that hall of feasting and of guests.   Along the walls shone hang-
ings wrought with gold, many wondrous sights for
all who gaze upon such things.   That bright house
had been greatly shattered, though all within was

[1] Unferth.

51

fast with iron bands. The hinges had been torn away. The roof alone was saved unhurt, when the monster, stained with wicked deeds, despairing of life, turned him to flight.

Death is not easily escaped, try it who will; but every living soul among the children of men dwelling upon the earth goeth of necessity unto his destined place, where the body, fast in its narrow bed, sleepeth after feast.[1]

Now the time was come for the son of Healfdene to go into the hall; the king himself was minded to partake of the feast. Never have I heard that that people in greater company gathered more bravely about their king. Then those happy men sat them down upon the benches; they rejoiced in the feasting. Their great-hearted kinsmen, Hrothgar and Hrothulf,[2] with fair courtesy quaffed many a bowl of mead in the high hall. Heorot was filled with friends. In that day the Scylding people had done no deeds of guile.

Then the son of Healfdene gave to Beowulf, in reward of victory, a golden ensign, a broidered

---

[1] This impressive, but irrelevant, passage is probably a bit of interpolation.

[2] Hrothgar's nephew, the Hrolf Kraki of Norse literature. His later quarrel with his uncle is prophetically hinted in the following sentences.

banner, a helmet, and a byrnie; many men saw a
mighty treasure-sword borne to the hero. Beowulf quaffed the cup in the hall. He needed not
to be ashamed before warriors of those sumptuous
gifts. Few have I heard of at the ale-bench who
gave to others in more friendly wise four treasures,
gold-adorned. About the crown of the helmet
there was a wreath all wrought with wires, which
protected the head, so that the tempered sword
could not greatly injure it, when the shielded warrior went out against his foe.

Moreover, the defence of heroes bade that eight
horses with golden bridles be led into the hall [1] under the barriers. Upon one of them there was a
saddle, cunningly wrought, adorned with jewels;—
it had been the battle-seat of the high king, when
the son of Healfdene was minded to take part in the
play of swords; [2] the might of the far-famed hero
failed never at the front, while the slain were fall-
ing. And then the prince of the Ingwines [3] gave
over to Beowulf the possession of these, both the
horses and the armor; bade him enjoy them well.
Thus, like a true man, did the great lord, the

---

[1] It is a common occurrence in old ballads and romances
to ride a horse directly into the hall. Cf. Malory's *Morte
Darthur*, 2. 3, *et passim*.

[2] War.   [3] Danes.

guardian of treasure and heroes, repay the storm of the fight with horses and treasure, so that none can dispraise them, none who wills to speak the truth aright.

XVI AND XVII

Hrothgar bestows gifts upon Beowulf's men. The bard sings the lay of King Finn.

AND moreover, the lord of heroes, at the mead-bench, bestowed a treasure, some heirloom, upon each of those who crossed the ocean-paths with Beowulf. And he bade that gold be paid for the man whom Grendel had wickedly slain,[1] as he would have slain more of them, had not all-knowing God and the hero's courage turned that fate from them; for the Lord ruled over all the children of men, even as now He doth; wherefore is understanding best in every place, and prudence of heart. He who long dwelleth in this world endureth much of good and evil in these days of strife.

There were singing and music blended together concerning Healfdene's battle-chieftain:[2] the harp

---

[1] So that Beowulf should not lose the weregild for his murdered man.

[2] Hnæf in the following tale.

was struck, a lay oft sung, when Hrothgar's bard
was to awaken joy in hall along the mead-bench.

THE LAY OF KING FINN

*How Hnaef of the Scyldings fell in an ancient feud with
Finn, king of the Eotens, he who had carried off his
sister, Hildeburh; and how Hengest, brother to Hnaef
and Hildeburh, made a treaty with Finn, and dwelt
with the Eotens for a season, until they feared him
and slew him. And of the last great fight when Finn
was slain; and how Queen Hildeburh was restored
to her people.*

Hnæf of the Scyldings, the hero of the Half-Danes,
was doomed to fall upon the Frisian slaughter-field at the
hands of the sons of Finn, what time the peril got hold on
them. Nor in truth did Hildeburh need to praise the
good faith of the Eotens; she, all blameless, was bereft
of her dear sons and brothers in the battle; wounded by
the spear they fell according to their fate—a sorrowful
woman she. Not without cause did the daughter of Hoc [1]
bewail Fate's decree when morn was come—when she beheld her murdered kinsmen beneath the sky, there where
she had erstwhile had the greatest of earth's joys. War
swept away all the thanes of Finn, save but a few, so that
he could nowise give battle to Hengest upon the field,
nor save by fighting the wretched remnant from the
prince's thane. But the Frisians offered Hengest terms:

[1] Hildeburh.

55

that they would fully prepare for him another great building, a hall and high throne, so that he might have equal
power with the sons of the Eotens, and that Finn, son of
Folcwald, would daily, at the giving of the gifts, do honor
to the Danes, would do honor to the troop of Hengest
with rings, with even as much costly treasure of plated
gold, as that wherewith he would rejoice the Frisians in
the mead-hall. Then on both sides they made a fast-
binding treaty of peace; Finn swore an oath unto Hengest, absolutely and unreservedly, that he would honorably
rule the sad remnant according to the decree of his councilors; so that no man there by word or deed should
break the pact, or ever do it violence by guileful craft,
although they, lordless men, followed the slayer of their
own prince, as they must do perforce; and if any of the
Frisians should with taunting words recall that feud,
then the edge of the sword was to avenge it. The oath
was sworn and massive gold was brought up from the
hoard.

The best of the warriors [1] among the Battle-Scyldings
was ready at the funeral pile; upon the pyre were clearly
to be seen the blood-stained sark, the swine of gold,[2] the
boar-helm iron-hard, and many a hero who had perished
of his wounds—these had fallen in the struggle. And
Hildeburh bade them commit her own son to the flames
at Hnæf's pyre, burn the body, laying it on the pile.
The hapless woman wept upon his shoulder, lamented
him in song. Uprose the warrior in the flame; the
greatest of funeral fires rolled upward to the clouds; it
roared before the mound. The heads were melted, the

[1] Hnæf.   [2] Cf. page 23.

56

gashes were burst open, the blood gushed forth from the wounds upon the body. Flame, that greediest of spirits, swallowed up all of both peoples whom war had snatched away. Gone was their glory.

Bereft of their friends, the warriors departed to their dwellings, to see Friesland, their homes, and high city. And Hengest dwelt with Finn all that blood-stained winter, wholly without strife; yet he was mindful of his native land, although he could not drive over the mere his ring-stemmed ship. The sea surged in the storm, fought with the wind. Winter locked the waves in its icy bond, till that a new year came unto the dwellings of earth, as still it doth, and the days gloriously bright which ever observe the season. Thus was the winter spent, and fair was the bosom of earth.

Then the exile [1] was minded to be gone; the guest departed from the courts. But he was thinking more of vengeance than of the sea-voyage, if haply he might bring to pass a deadly conflict and so commemorate the sons of the Eotens. Therefore he escaped not the lot of mortals when the son of Hunlaf thrust into his breast the flashing sword, best of blades; wherefore its edges were well known among the Eotens. Likewise, thereafter, dire death by the sword befell the brave-hearted Finn in his own home, when Guthlaf and Oslaf, after the sea-journey, mournfully lamented the fierce struggle—blamed him for their share of sorrow. He could not retain the wavering spirit within his breast.

And the hall was covered with the bodies of foemen, and King Finn, likewise, was slain in the midst of his

[1] Hengest.

57

guardsmen, and the queen was taken. The Scylding warriors bore to their ships all the possessions of the king of the land—whatever they could find in Finn's home of jewels and curious gems. They bore the noble lady over the sea-paths to the land of the Danes, led her to her people.

The lay was sung, the gleeman's tale was ended. Mirth rose high again, clear sounded the noise of revelry. The cup-bearers poured out wine from wondrous vessels. And Wealhtheow came forth with a crown of gold upon her head, and went to where were seated uncle and nephew, those two good friends;—as yet there was peace between them, each to the other true.[1] There also sat Unferth, the spokesman, at the feet of the lord of the Scyldings; every man of them trusted his spirit, yea, and that he had good courage, although he dealt not uprightly with his kinsmen in the play of swords.[2]

And the lady of the Scyldings spoke: "Take this cup, my sovereign lord, giver of treasure. Rejoice, thou prince of the people, and speak kind words unto the Geats, as is well-fitting. Be gracious toward the Geats and mindful of gifts; for now thou hast peace both far and near. It has

[1] See page 52 and note 2.
[2] See Beowulf's charge against him, page 35.

been told me that thou wouldst gladly have this warrior for a son. Heorot, the bright gift-hall, is cleansed. Give, then, while thou mayst, many rewards, and bequeath people and realm to thy kinsmen, when thou must go hence unto the appointed doom. I know that my gracious Hrothulf will honorably rule the youth,[1] if thou, lord of the Scyldings, leave the world ere he. I think that he will requite our offspring well, if he bethink him of our benefits toward him in time past, when he was a child, of all that we did for his pleasure and honor."

Then she turned to where her sons were sitting, Hrethric and Hrothmund, and the offspring of heroes, all the youth together; and there by the two brothers sat that brave man, Beowulf the Geat.

XVIII

The queen giveth gifts to Beowulf, and a fair collar which King Hygelac wore in aftertime. They feast, and the heroes rest in Heorot.

A CUP was borne to him, and friendly greeting offered, and twisted gold graciously presented him: two armlets, rings, and armor, and the goodliest of collars I have ever heard of upon earth. Never

---

[1] Act as regent.

heard I of a fairer among the treasured jewels of
heroes beneath the sky, ne'er since Hama bore
away to the bright city the collar of the Brisings,[1]
the fair gem and its casket; he fled the cunning
snares of Eormanric, and chose everlasting gain.[2]
This ring had Hygelac, the Geat, grandson of
Swerting, on his last raid,[3] when, beneath his banner, he defended his treasure and guarded the
plunder of battle. Wyrd took him away, when he,
foolhardy, suffered woe in feud with the Frisians;
for that mighty chieftain bore the jewel with its
precious stones over the arching sea; and he fell
beneath his shield. Then the body of the king
came into the possession of the Franks, his breast-
mail, and the jewel, too; meaner warriors stripped
the body after the slaughter of battle; the corpses
of the Geats were strewed upon the field.

[1] Beowulf's collar is compared to the famous Brising
necklace, which, according to the *Elder Edda*, is the property of the goddess Freya; apparently it later came into
the possession of Hermanric the Ostrogoth (Eormanric),
from whom it was stolen by one Hama. The later history
of Beowulf's jewel follows, somewhat after the manner of
the Homeric account of Agamemnon's sceptre.

[2] Probably entered a monastery.

[3] One of the few authentic historical allusions in the
poem. The account of the raid of "Chochilaicus"
(Hygelac) may be found in the *Historia Francorum* of
Gregory of Tours. The event occurred about 512
A.D.

The hall resounded. Wealhtheow spoke before
the host and said: "Receive with joy this collar,
dear Beowulf, beloved youth, and use this armor
—treasures of our people—and prosper well; show
thyself strong; and be kind in thy counsel to these
youths. I will be mindful of thy reward. Thou
hast brought it to pass that men shall give thee
honor evermore, in all the earth, far as the sea en-
compasseth its windswept walls. Be, while thou
livest, a prosperous prince; much treasure truly I
wish thee. Be thou friendly to my son, guarding
his happy state.[1] Here is each hero true to the
other, gentle of spirit, and loyal to his lord; the
thanes are obedient, the people ready at call. Ye
warriors, cheered with wine, do as I bid ye."

Then she went to her seat. There was the
choicest of feasts; the men drank wine. They
knew not Wyrd, cruel destiny, as it had gone forth
of old unto many a hero.

When even was come, and Hrothgar, the ruler,
had departed to his lodge unto his evening rest,
countless heroes guarded the house as they had oft
of yore. They made bare the bench and spread
upon it beds and pillows. Doomed and nigh unto

[1] Probably in case of his father's death, which she re-
ferred to a moment since.

61

death, one of the revelers laid him down to rest in
the hall. At their heads they placed their battle-
shields, bright bucklers. There upon the bench
above each hero were clearly to be seen the towering helm, the ringèd coat of mail, the mighty spear.
It was their wont to be ever ready for battle,
whether at home or in the field, ready for either,
even at the moment when their chief had need
of them. That was a good people.

PART II

BEOWULF AND GRENDEL'S MOTHER

XIX

Grendel's mother cometh to avenge her son. She seizes Æschere in Heorot.

THEN they sank to sleep. But one paid dearly for his evening rest, as had often happened when Grendel haunted that gold-hall and wrought evil till his end came, death for his sins. It now became evident to men that, though the foe was dead, there yet lived for a long time after the fierce combat, an avenger—Grendel's mother. The witch, woman-monster, brooded over her woes, she who was doomed to dwell among the terrors of the waters, in the cold streams, from the time when Cain slew with the sword his only brother, his own father's son; then he departed, banished, marked with murder, fleeing from the joys of men and dwelt in the wilderness. From him there woke to life many Fate-sent demons. One of these was Grendel,[1] a fierce wolf, full of hatred. But he had found at Heorot a man on the watch, waiting to give him battle. Then the monster grappled with him, but Beowulf bethought him of his mighty strength, the gift of God, and in Him as the Almighty he trusted for favor, for help and succor; in this trust he overcame the fiend, laid low that spirit of hell. Then Grendel, enemy to mankind, went forth joyless to behold the abode of death. But his mother, still wroth and ravenous, determined to go a sad journey to avenge the death of her son; and she came to Heorot, where the Ring-Danes lay asleep about the hall. Straightway terror fell upon the heroes once again when Grendel's mother burst in upon them. But the fear was less than in the time of Grendel, even as the strength of maids, or a woman's rage in war, is less than an armed man's, what time the hilted sword, hammer-forged, stained with blood, cleaves with keen blade the boar on foeman's helmet. There above the benches in the hall the hard-edged sword was

---

[1] This repetition of the events of the earlier part may serve to show that the author was conscious of his transition to a new subject. It is even possible that the recitation of the story may sometimes have begun at or near this point.

drawn, and many a shield upreared, fast in the hand; none thought of helm or broad corslet when the terror got hold of him. She was in haste, for she was discovered; she wished to get thence with her life. Of a sudden she clutched one of the heroes, and was off to the fen. The mighty warrior, the famed hero whom the hag murdered in his sleep, was the dearest to Hrothgar of all the men in his band of comrades between the seas. Beowulf was not there; for another lodging-place had been assigned to the mighty Geat after the giving of treasure. A cry arose in Heorot. All in its gore she had taken the famous arm;[1] sorrow was renewed in the dwellings. No good exchange was that which cost both peoples the lives of friends.

Then the old king, the hoary warrior, was sad at heart when he learned that his chief thane had lost his life, that his dearest friend was dead. Straightway Beowulf, the hero blessed with victory, was brought to the bower; the prince, the noble warrior, went at daybreak with his comrades to where the prudent king was waiting to know if perchance the Almighty would ever work a happy change for him, after grievous tidings. And the hero, famed in war, strode up the hall with his

[1] Grendel's; see page 50.

65

band of thanes—while loud the room resounded—
to greet the wise lord of the Ingwines; he asked
if his night had been restful, as he had wished.

XX

*Hrothgar lamenteth for Æschere. He tells Beowulf of the
monster and her haunt.*

HROTHGAR, defence of the Scyldings, spoke:
"Ask not after bliss,—sorrow in hall is renewed
for the Danish folk. Æschere is dead, Yrmen-
laf's elder brother, my councilor and my adviser,
who stood by me, shoulder to shoulder, when we
warded our heads in battle, while hosts rushed
together and helmets crashed. Like Æschere
should every noble be—an excellent hero. He
was slain in Heorot by a restless destroyer.

"I know not whither the awful monster, exulting in her prey, has turned her homeward steps,
rejoicing in her fill. She has avenged the strife
in which thou slewest Grendel yesternight, grappling fiercely with him, for that he too long had
wasted and destroyed my people. He fell in the
fight, forfeiting his life, and now another is come,
a mighty and a deadly foe, thinking to avenge her
son. She has carried the feud further; wherefore

it may well seem a heavy woe to many a thane who grieveth in spirit for his treasure-giver. Low lies the hand which did satisfy all your desires.

"I have heard the people dwelling in my land, hall-rulers, say that they had often seen two such mighty stalkers of the marches, spirits of other-where, haunting the moors. One of them, as they could know full well, was like unto a woman; the other miscreated being, in the image of man wandered in exile (save that he was larger than any man), whom in the olden time the people named Grendel. They knew not if he ever had a father among the spirits of darkness. (They dwell in a hidden land amid wolf-haunted slopes and savage fen-paths, the wind-swept cliffs where the mountain-stream falleth, shrouded in the mists of the headlands, its flood flowing under-ground. It is not far thence in measure of miles that the mere lieth. Over it hang groves in hoary whiteness; a forest with fixed roots bendeth over the waters. There in the night-tide is a dread wonder seen—a fire on the flood. There is none of the children of men so wise that he knoweth the depths thereof. Although hard pressed by hounds, the heath-ranging stag, with mighty horns, may seek out that forest, driven from afar, yet

67

sooner will he yield up life and breath upon the bank than hide his head within its waters.   Cheerless is the place.   Thence the surge riseth, wan to the clouds, when the winds stir up foul weather, till the air thicken and the heavens weep.)

"Now once again help rests with thee alone. Thou knowest not yet the spot, the savage place where thou mayst find the sinful creature.   Seek it out, if thou dare.   I will reward thee, as I did before, with olden treasures and with twisted gold, if thou get thence alive."

XXI

They track Grendel's mother to the mere.   Beowulf slayeth a sea-monster.

THEN spoke Beowulf, son of Ecgtheow: "Sorrow not, thou wise man.   It is better for a man to avenge his friend than mourn exceedingly. Each of us must abide the end of the worldly life, wherefore let him who may, win glory ere he die; thus shall it be best for a warrior when life is past. Arise, O guardian of the kingdom, let us straightway go and look upon the tracks of Grendel's dam.   I promise thee this: she shall not escape to the covert, neither into the bosom of the earth,

68

nor to mountain-wood, nor to the bottom of the
sea, go where she will. This day do thou bear
in patience every woe of thine, as I expect of thee."

Then the old man leapt up and thanked God,
the mighty Lord, for what that man had said.
And they bridled Hrothgar's horse, a steed with
curling mane. The wise prince rode stately forth,
and with him fared a troop of shielded warriors.
Footprints were clearly seen along the forest-path,
her track across the land. She had gone forth,
over the murky moor, and borne away lifeless that
best of thanes, who with Hrothgar ruled the hall.

And the offspring of princes went over steep and
rocky slopes and narrow ways, straight lonely
passes, an unknown course; over sheer cliffs and
many a sea-beast's haunt. He, with a few prudent men, went on before to view the spot, until
he suddenly came upon mountain-trees o'erhang-
ing the gray rock—a cheerless wood. Beneath it
lay a water, bloody and troubled. All the Danes,
all the friends of the Scyldings, each hero and many
a thane, sad at heart then suffered sore distress;
for there upon the sea-cliff they found the head
of Æschere. The waters were seething with blood
and hot gore—the people gazed.

At times the horn sang out an eager lay. All

the troop sat down. They saw in the water many of the serpent kind, strange dragons swimming the deep. Likewise they saw sea-monsters lying along the headland-slopes, serpents and wild beasts, such as oft at morning-tide make a journey, fraught with sorrow, over the sail-road. They sped away, bitter and swollen with wrath, when they heard the sound, the song of the battle-horn. But the lord of the Geats with bow and arrow took the life of one of them, as it buffeted the waves, so that the hard shaft pierced the vitals; he was then the slower in swimming the sea, for death seized him. Straightway he was hard pressed with the sharp barbs of hookèd spears, fiercely attacked, and drawn up on the cliff, a wondrous wave-tosser. The men looked on the strange and grisly beast.

Then Beowulf girded him with noble armor; he took no thought for his life. His byrnie, hand-woven, broad, and of many colors, was to search out the deeps. This armor could well protect his body so that the grip of the foe could not harm his breast, nor the clutch of the angry beast do aught against his life. Moreover, the white helmet guarded his head, even that which was to plunge into the depths of the mere, passing through the tumult of the waters; it was all decked with gold, encircled with noble chains, as the weapon-smith wrought it in days of yore; wondrously he made it, and set it about with boar-figures so that no brand nor battle-sword could bite it.[1]

Nor was that the least of his mighty aids which Hrothgar's spokesman [2] lent him in his need—the name of the hilted sword was Hrunting, and it was one of the greatest among olden treasures; its blade was of iron, stained with poison-twigs, hardened with blood of battle; it had never failed any man whose hand had wielded it in fight, any who durst go on perilous adventures to the field of battle—it was not the first time that it had need to do high deeds.   Surely when the son of Ecglaf,[2] strong in his might, lent that weapon to a better swordsman, he did not remember what he had aid when drunk with wine; as for him, he dursts not risk his life beneath the warring waves and do a hero's deeds; there he lost the glory, the fame of valor.   It was not so with the other when he had armed him for the fight.

[1] See page 23, note 1.   [2] Unferth.

71

XXII

Beowulf bids farewell to Hrothgar and plunges into the mere. The monster seizes upon him. They fight.

THEN spoke Beowulf, son of Ecgtheow: "Remember, thou great son of Healfdene, wise chieftain, gracious friend of men, now that I am ready for this exploit, what we two spoke of aforetime; that, if I must needs lose my life for thee, thou wouldst ever be as a father to me when I was gone hence. Guard thou my thanes, my own comrades, if the fight take me, and do thou also send unto Hygelac the treasures that thou gavest me, beloved Hrothgar. Then, when the son of Hrethel, lord of the Geats, shall look upon that treasure, he may behold and see by the gold that I found a bountiful benefactor, and enjoyed these gifts while I might. And do thou let Unferth, that far-famed man, have the old heirloom, the wondrous wavy sword of tempered blade. I will win glory with Hrunting, or death shall take me."

After these words the lord of the Weder-Geats boldly made haste; he would await no answer, but the surging waters swallowed up the warrior.

It was the space of a day ere he got sight of the bottom.

Soon the blood-thirsty creature, she who had lived for a hundred seasons, grim and greedy, in the waters' flow, found that one was there from above seeking out the abode of monsters. She seized upon the warrior and clutched him with her horrid claws; nevertheless she did no harm to his sound body, for the ringèd armor girt him round about, so that she could not pierce the byrnie, the linkèd coat of mail, with her hateful fingers. Then the mere-wolf, when she came to the bottom, bore the ring-prince to her dwelling, so that he could nowise wield his weapons, brave though he was; for many monsters came at him, many a sea-beast with awful tusks broke his battle-sark—the evil creatures pressed him hard.

Then the hero saw that he was in some dreadful hall, where the water could not harm him a whit; the swift clutch of the current could not touch him, because of the roofed hall. He saw a fire-light, a gleaming flame brightly shining. Then the hero got sight of the mighty mere-woman—the she-wolf of the deep. He made at her fiercely with his war-sword. His hand did not refuse the blow, so that the ringèd blade sang out a greedy war-song

73

on her head. But the stranger found that the gleaming sword would make no wound, nor harm her life; so the blade failed the prince at need. It had aforetime endured many a hard fight, had often cleft the helmet and the byrnie of the doomed; this was the first time that the precious treasure ever failed of its glory. Yet the kinsman of Hygelac, heedful of great deeds, was steadfast of purpose, not faltering in courage. Then the angry warrior threw from him the carved sword, strong and steel-edged, studded with jewels, and it lay upon the ground. He trusted to his strength, to the mighty grip of his hand. So must a brave man do when he thinketh to win lasting praise in war— he taketh no thought for his life.

Then the lord of the War-Geats, shrinking not from the fight, seized Grendel's mother by the shoulder, and full of wrath, the valiant in battle threw his deadly foe so that she fell to the floor. Speedily she paid him his reward again with fierce grapplings and clutched at him, and being wearied, he stumbled and fell, he, the champion, strongest of warriors. Then she leapt and sat upon him, and drew her dagger, broad and brown-edged, to avenge her son, her only offspring. But on his shoulder lay his woven coat of mail; it saved his

life, barring the entrance against point and blade.
Then the son of Ecgtheow, chief of the Geats,
would have perished beneath the sea-bottom,
had not his byrnie, his hard war-shirt aided him,
and Holy God, the wise Lord, brought victory to
pass, the King of heaven easily adjudging it aright.
Thereafter he stood up again.

XXIII

*Beowulf lays hold upon a giant sword and slays the evil
beast. He finds Grendel's dead body and cuts off the
head, and swims up to his thanes upon the shore. They
go back to Heorot.*

THEN he saw among the armor a victorious
blade, an old sword of the giant-age, keen-edged,
the glory of warriors; it was the choicest of weapons—save that it was larger than any other man
was able to carry into battle—good, and splendidly
wrought, for it was the work of the giants. And
the warrior of the Scyldings seized the belted hilt;
savage and angry, he drew forth the ring-sword,
and, hopeless of life, smote so fiercely that the hard
sword caught her by the neck, breaking the ring-
bones; the blade drove right through her doomed
body, and she sank upon the floor. The sword was
bloody; the hero exulted in his deed.

75

The flame burst forth; light filled the place, even as when the candle of heaven is shining brightly from the sky. He gazed about the place and turned him to the wall; the thane of Hygelac, angry and resolute, lifted the great weapon by the hilts. The blade was not worthless to the warrior, for he wished to repay Grendel straightway for the many attacks which he had made upon the West-Danes —oftener far than once—what time he slew Hrothgar's hearth-companions in their slumber and devoured fifteen of the sleeping Danes and carried off as many more, a horrid prey. The fierce warrior had given him his reward, so that he now saw Grendel lying lifeless in his resting-place, spent with his fight, so deadly had the combat been for him in Heorot. The body bounded far when it suffered a blow after death, a mighty sword-stroke. And thus he smote off the head.

Soon the prudent men who were watching the mere with Hrothgar saw that the surging waves were all troubled, and the water mingled with blood. The old men, white-haired, talked together of the hero, how they thought that the prince would never come again to their great lord, exultant in victory; for many believed that the sea-wolf had rent him in pieces.

Then came the ninth hour of the day. The bold Scyldings left the cliff, the bounteous friend of men departed to his home. But the strangers sat there, sick at heart, and gazed upon the mere; they longed but did not ever think to see their own dear lord again.

Meanwhile the sword,⟨ that war-blade, being drenched with blood, began to waste away in icicles of steel; it melted wondrously like ice when the Father looseneth the frost, unwindeth the ropes that bind the waves;⟩He who ruleth the times and seasons, He is a God of righteousness. The lord of the Weder-Geats took no treasure from that hall, although he saw much there, none save the head, and the hilt bright with gold; the blade had melted, the graven sword had burned away, so hot had been the blood, so venomous the strange spirit that had perished there.

Soon he was swimming off, he who had survived the onset of his foes; he plunged up through the water. The surging waves were cleansed, the wide expanse where that strange spirit had laid down her life and the fleeting days of this world.

And the defence of seamen came to land, stoutly swimming; he rejoiced in his sea-spoil, the great burden that he bore with him. And his valiant band of thanes went unto him, giving thanks to God; they rejoiced in their chief, for that they could see him safe and sound. Then they quickly loosed helm and byrnie from the valiant man. The mere grew calm, but the water beneath the clouds was stained with the gore of battle.

They set forth along the foot-path glad at heart; the men, kingly bold, measured the earth-ways, the well-known roads. They bore away the head from the sea-cliff—a hard task for all those men, great-hearted as they were; four of them must needs bear with toil that head of Grendel upon a spear to the gold-hall. And forthwith the fourteen Geats, bold and warlike, came to the hall, and their brave lord in their midst trod the meadows. And the chief of the thanes, the valiant man crowned with glory, the warrior brave in battle, went in to greet Hrothgar. And Grendel's head was borne by the hair into the hall where the men were drinking—a terror alike to heroes and to queen.[1] The people gazed upon that wondrous sight.

[1] Cf. *Sir Andrew Barton*, 80–81.

XXIV AND XXV

Beowulf tells of his fight, and Hrothgar discourses. They feast in Heorot. In the morning the Geats make ready to depart.

BEOWULF, son of Ecgtheow, spoke: "Behold, O son of Healfdene, lord of the Scyldings, we have joyfully brought thee this sea-spoil which here thou lookest on, a token of glory. Hardly did I escape with my life; painfully fighting under the waters, I ventured on the work. The struggle would have well-nigh failed me, had not God shielded me. Nor could I do aught with Hrunting in the fight, though that be a good weapon; but the Ruler of the people—full often hath He guided friendless men—granted that I saw an old and mighty sword hanging all beauteous on the wall; so I drew that weapon forth. And I slew ın fight the keepers of that house, for occasion favored me. But the war-sword, the graven blade, burned away when the blood gushed forth, hottest of battle-gore. The hilt I bore away from the enemy, avenging, as was meet, their crimes, the slaughter of the Danes. I promise thee that thou, with a troop of thy men, mayst sleep in Heorot free from care, thou and all the thanes of thy people, young and old; thou needest not fear death for them from that quarter, as formerly thou didst, O lord of the Scyldings."

Then the golden hilt, the ancient work of giants, was given into the hands of the agèd warrior, the hoary leader in battle. After the fall of the devils, this work of cunning smiths came into the possession of the lord of the Danes; when the fierce-hearted enemy of God, guilty of murder, quitted this world, he and his mother too, it passed into the keeping of the best of kings between the seas, the best of those who gave out gifts of money in the Danish land.

Hrothgar spoke; he looked upon the hilt, the old heirloom on which was graven the beginning of the ancient strife, what time the flood, the rushing ocean, destroyed the giant race.[1] They had behaved frowardly. That people was estranged from the eternal Lord; wherefore the Ruler gave them their final reward in the flood of waters. And on the guard of shining gold was rightly graven, set forth and told in runic letters, for whom the sword had first been made, that best of blades, with its twisted hilt brightly adorned with snakes.

[1] *Genesis* 4, 1.

Then the wise son of Healfdene spoke—silent
were they all: "Lo! the agèd ruler who remem-
bereth far-off days, he who doeth righteousness
and truth among the people, may say that this
hero was born of the nobler stock. The fame of
thee, my friend Beowulf, is spread abroad among
every people far and wide. Thou dost hold it all
with meekness; yea, all thy might with prudence
of mind. I will make good my compact with
thee, even as we did agree aforetime. Thou
shalt be a lasting comfort to thy people, a help to
warriors.

"Not so was Heremod [1] to the children of Ecgwela, the Honor-Scyldings. He throve not for
their welfare, but became the destruction and the
deadly plague of the Danish people; for in his rage
he slew his table-companions, the friends of his
bosom, until he, the great prince, went forth alone,
far from the joys of men. Although mighty God
advanced him and set him above all men in strength
and in the joys of power, yet there grew up a blood-
thirsty spirit in his heart; he gave no treasure to
the Danes, as was meet, so that he lived joyless,
suffering punishment for his hostility in the lasting
wretchedness of his people. Learn thou from this;

[1] See page 48, and note 1.

lay hold upon manly virtue. With the wisdom of many winters I have told this tale for thee.

"Wonderful it is to tell how mighty God, in His great spirit, giveth wisdom unto mankind and land and noble rank. He ruleth over all. But at times He letteth the thoughts of a man's heart stray toward the satisfaction of his own desires; He giveth him worldly joys in his fatherland, a fenced city of men to hold; He maketh whole regions of the earth subject unto him, a wide domain, so that in his blindness he considereth not his end. He dwelleth in plenty; no whit doth sickness or age beset him; sorrow darkeneth not his spirit; nowhere doth strife appear, or deadly hate; but all the world moveth to his will.

"He knoweth no worse state, until at length much pride grows and flourishes within him, while the watchman is sleeping, the keeper of the soul. Too deep is that slumber, encompassed with sorrows; the Adversary is at hand, who shooteth from his bow in evil wise; and the helmeted man is smitten in the breast with a bitter arrow, being unable to ward off the crooked counsels of the Accursèd Spirit. Too little seemeth that which he hath long possessed. He is covetous in his froward heart; he doth not gloryingly bestow the

82

plated rings, and he forgetteth and despiseth the future, by reason of the bounteous honors which God, the King of glory, hath accorded him.

"But in the end it is brought to pass that the failing body wasteth away; and falleth doomed. Another succeedeth, one who giveth out the treasure, nothing loath, the prince's store of riches laid up of old—naught to fear hath he.

"Keep thee from deadly envy, then, beloved Beowulf, best of men, and choose thou the better course, everlasting gain. Incline thee not to pride, O mighty warrior. Now the flower of thy strength lasteth for a season, but soon sickness or sword shall cut thee off from thy strength, or the embrace of fire, or the surge of the flood, or the stab of the sword, or the flight of the spear, or wretched age; or else the light of thine eyes shall fail and grow dim, and forthwith death shall overcome thee, O noble hero.

"Thus I ruled over the Ring-Danes fifty years beneath the sky, and defended them in battle with spear and sword from many a tribe throughout the world; insomuch that I thought I had no foe beneath the breadth of heaven. Lo! all this was changed for me in my land; joy changed to sorrow, when Grendel, my foe of old, fell upon my home.

Ever in my heart I suffered great sorrow because of this persecution. Wherefore thanks be to God, our everlasting Lord, that I have lived to see with mine eyes this gory head, now the old strife is over.

"Go now to thy seat, honored warrior, partake in the joy of the feasting. Thou and I will share full many treasures when morning is come."

The Geat was glad at heart, and went straightway to his seat, as the wise king bade him. Then once again a fair feast was made ready as before for those brave men in the hall.

The helm of night loured dark over the warriors. All the company arose; the agèd man, the gray-haired Scylding, was minded to go to his bed. And the Geat, the brave shield-warrior, had an exceeding great desire of rest. Forthwith the hall-thane, he who duly supplied all the warrior's needs, such as seafarers must have in that day, guided forth that traveler from afar, wearied with his venture. And the great-hearted hero rested him.

The hall towered aloft, vast and gold-adorned. The guest slept within, until the black raven, blithe of heart, announced the joy of heaven, and the bright sun came gliding over earth. The warriors hastened, the heroes longed to be return-

84

ing to their people; the great-hearted guest wished
to take ship and go far thence.

And the hero bade the son of Ecglaf [1] bear away
Hrunting, bade him take the sword, belovèd weapon; he thanked him for lending it, said that he
counted it a good war-friend, a mighty in battle;
he uttered no word in blame of that edged sword
—he was a great-hearted man!

And when the warriors, eager for the voyage,
were ready armed, the chief, dear in the sight of the
Danes, went to the throne where the other was; the
hero, bold in battle, gave greeting to Hrothgar.

XXVI

*Beowulf bids farewell to Hrothgar and the aged king weeps
at his departure. He giveth him many treasures. The
Geats go down to the sea.*

BEOWULF, son of Ecgtheow, spoke: "Now we
seafarers, travelers from afar, would say that we
purpose to return unto Hygelac. We have been
well entertained here to our heart's desire: thou
hast been good to us. If, then, O lord of men, I can
win upon earth more of thy heart's love than I have
yet done, I shall be ready at once for warlike deeds.

[1] Unferth.

85

If I learn beyond the course of the waters that thy neighbors beset thee sore, as did thine enemies in days gone by, I will bring a thousand thanes and warriors to help thee. I know that Hygelac, lord of the Geats, shepherd of the people, young though he be, will further me by word and deed that I may do honor to thee and bring to thine aid the shafted spear and the succor of my strength, when thou hast need of men. Moreover, if Hrethric, the king's son, take service at the Geatish court,[1] he will find there many friends; far countries are best sought out by him who is strong within himself."

Hrothgar spoke and answered him again: "The all-knowing Lord hath sent these words into thy mind; I never heard one so young in life speak more wisely. Thou art strong in thy might, and prudent of mind, wise in thy discourse. I count it likely that, if ever the spear or fierce warfare or sickness or weapon take away thy lord, the heir of Hrethel, shepherd of the people, and if thou be yet alive, the Sea-Geats will have none better to choose as king, as guardian of treasure and heroes, if haply thou be willing to govern the kingdom of

---

[1] Cf. *Germania* 14: "Si civitas in qua orti sunt, longa pace et otio torpeat, plerique nobilium adulescentium petunt ultro eas nationes quae tum bellum aliquod gerunt," and the rest.

thy folk.   Thy great heart delighteth me more and
more, dear Beowulf.   Thou hast brought it to pass
that there shall be peace between our people, the
Geat folk and the Spear-Danes; and strife shall
cease, the evil feuds which they have endured in
time past.   We shall have treasure in common
while I rule over this wide realm; many friends
shall greet one another with good things across the
gannet's bath; [1] the ringèd ship shall bring gifts
and love-tokens over the sea.   I know that the
peoples are firmly united toward friend and toward
foe, blameless in every way, after the olden cus-
toms."

And moreover the son of Healfdene, shelter of
warriors, gave unto him twelve treasures within
the hall; he bade him go in safety with these gifts
unto his own dear people, and quickly come again.
And the king of noble lineage, lord of the Scyldings,
kissed that best of thanes and clasped him round
the neck; tears fell from the gray-haired man.   The
wise and aged king looked for either thing,[2] but
rather for the second, that they would never meet
again, brave in the council.   The hero was so dear

[1] The sea.
[2] A knotty passage, perhaps corrupt.   There were two
possibilities, the passage seems to imply: that Hrothgar
might see Beowulf again, and that he might not.

to him that he could not contain his welling grief, for in his breast secret longing after the dear man, fast bound within his heart, burned through his blood.

Then Beowulf, the warrior proud of his gold, exulting in his treasure, went thence treading the grassy plain. The ship awaited her lord, riding at anchor. And, as they went, Hrothgar's gift was praised full oft. He was a king, blameless in every wise, until old age, which has often wasted many a man, took from him the joys of strength.

XXVII

Beowulf presents to the coast-warden a golden sword. The Geats return unto their land. They bear the treasures to the hall where dwells King Hygelac with his queen, Hygd. The tale of Thrytho told.

THEN the band of brave retainers came to the sea; they wore ringèd armor, woven shirts of mail. The land-warden beheld the heroes when they came again, even as he had done before. But not with insult did he greet the guests from the peak of the cliff, but rode toward them, as they came unto their ship, saying that the Weder people, the bright-coated warriors, were welcome.

Then the spacious bark, the ring-stemmed ship upon the beach, was laden with the armor, with the horses and the treasures; the mast towered high over the wealth from Hrothgar's hoard. Beowulf gave to the boat-warden a sword all bound with gold, so that he was the more honored thereafter at the mead-bench because of that treasure and heirloom.

And he departed in his ship, driving the deep waters asunder; he left the Danish land. Then a sail, one of the sea-cloths, was fastened to the mast. The sea-craft groaned. The wind blowing over the waters did not drive the bark from her course; the ship sailed on: with wreathèd prow she floated forth, foamy-necked, over the waters of the sea, until the men could descry the Geatish cliffs, the well-known headlands. The keel, driven by the wind, bounded up, and stood ashore. Straightway the harbor-guard was ready at the water's edge, he who upon the beach had long been looking out afar, eager for the dear men. He bound the broad-bosomed ship with anchor-ropes fast to the shore, lest the force of the waves should drive the fair boat away.

And Beowulf bade them bear up ashore the princely treasure, the jewels and the beaten gold.

It was not far thence for them to go unto the giver of treasure, Hygelac, son of Hrethel ; there at home he dwells with his companions, nigh the sea-wall.

Fair was the house; its lord a brave king, great in hall. Hygd, daughter of Hæreth, was very young, was wise and well nurtured, although she had lived but few winters within the castle walls; yet she was not mean-spirited, and nowise sparing in gifts of precious treasures to the Geats.

THE TALE OF THRYTHO

Much unlike Hygd was a queen named Thrytho, proud and wrathful, until Offa subdued her.

Thrytho,[1] the fierce queen of the people, showed forth wrath and evil dire; no brave man among the dear comrades durst venture by day to look upon her with his eyes, none save her lord; else he might count on deadly bonds, hand-woven, being destined for him. Straightway after his seizure the sword was appointed for use, so that the carved weapon might decide it, and tell forth the baleful murder. Such is no queenly custom for a woman to practice, peerless though she be—that a weaver of peace [2]

[1] This account of Thrytho is apparently introduced to contrast her with Hygd; so Beowulf (pages 48, 81) was praised by contrast with Heremod.

[2] This kenning for a queen is significant in many ways.

should attempt the life of a dear retainer because of pre-
tended insult.

But the kinsman of Hemming [1] checked this. The ale-
drinkers told another story, how that she wrought less
evil to the people, fewer deeds of hate after she was given,
all gold-adorned, to the young warrior of noble lineage,
when she at her father's bidding, journeyed over the dark
waters unto Offa's hall. There, while she lived, she enjoyed her destiny upon the throne, famed for her good-
ness. She held high love toward the prince of heroes
who, as I have heard, was the best of all mankind between the seas, best of all the race of men on earth.
Therefore Offa, bold with the spear, was honored far and
wide for gifts and warfare. Wisely he ruled his native
land. From him sprang Eomær, kinsman of Hemming,
grandson of Garmund, skilful in warfare, for the help
of heroes.

XXVIII

*Beowulf is received by Hygelac, and telleth of his meeting
with Grendel. Of Freawaru.*

THEN the brave chief went forth over the sands
with his companions, treading the sea-beach, the
wide-stretching shores. The candle of the world
was shining, the sun in its course beaming from the
south. They went their ways; boldly betook them
to where, as they had heard, the young and gracious

[1] Offa.

war-king, shelter of heroes, slayer of Ongentheow,[1] was giving out rings within his city. Speedily Beowulf's coming was announced to Hygelac, how that the shelter of warriors, his shield-comrade, was come back alive to the hall, come back to the court, safe from combat. Straightway the hall within was made ready for the travelers, even as the ruler bade.

Then he who had scaped from the strife sat by the king himself, kinsman by kinsman, after his lord with courtly speech had greeted the loyal hero with mighty words. And Hæreth's daughter passed about the hall, pouring out the mead; for she loved the people; she bore the mead-cup to the hands of the heroes.

Then Hygelac began to question his companions full fairly in the lofty hall, for he was spurred with longing to know touching the adventures of the Sea-Geats: "How fared ye in your journeying, dear Beowulf, when thou on a sudden didst resolve to seek combat far away over the salt waters, battle in Heorot? Didst thou in aught lessen the well-known woe of Hrothgar, the mighty lord? I have

[1] See page 133, where we are told that Ongentheow was slain by Eofor, one of Hygelac's men. It is proper for the retainer to attribute his glory to his lord. See *Agricola* 8, and *Germania* 14.

nourished brooding care and sorrow in my heart, for I put no trust in the journey of my belovèd thane. Long did I entreat thee not to attack the deadly beast, but let the South-Danes themselves put an end to their strife with Grendel. I give thanks unto God that I am suffered to see thee safe."

Beowulf, son of Ecgtheow, spoke: "Known unto many, my lord Hygelac, is the famous meeting 'twixt Grendel and me, and our fighting there on the field where he had wrought much sorrow for the Victor-[1]Scyldings and misery evermore. All that I avenged, so that none of Grendel's kin on earth need boast of that fray at twilight, not even he of the loathèd race who shall live the longest in the midst of the moorland.

"When I came into that country, I went first into the ring-hall to greet Hrothgar. Straightway the great kinsman of Healfdene, when he knew my mind, gave me a seat with his own son. It was a joyous host; I have never seen greater joy at the mead among any hall-guests beneath the vault of heaven. At times the great queen, the peace and bond of peoples,[2] passed all about the hall, and

---

[1] The epithet is here either purely formal (cf. page 36, note 2), or touched with sarcasm.   [2] Cf. page 90, and note 2.

cheered the hearts of the young retainers; oft-times she gave a ring to some warrior ere she went to her seat. At times Hrothgar's daughter bore the ale-cup before the nobles, unto the warriors in order. I heard those in the hall call her Freawaru as she gave studded treasure to the heroes."

FREAWARU [1]

How Freawaru, daughter to Hrothgar, is betrothed to Ingeld of the Heathobards, they who were Hrothgar's enemies of old. And how Ingeld will be provoked to the murder of a thane who attends on Freawaru; and how Ingeld's love for that lady will wane.

"Young and gold-adorned, she is promised to the glad son of Froda; this has seemed good to the lord of the Scyldings, defender of the kingdom, and he counts it a gain—by this marriage to allay many deadly feuds and strifes. Yet, oft and not rarely, in any place after a prince has fallen, it is but a little time that the deadly spear lies at rest, fair though the bride may be.

"Wherefore it may well displease the lord of the Heathobards and all the thanes of that people when he goes into hall with his lady, that his warriors attend on

[1] This episode, a fine piece of epic prophecy, refers to a tale probably well known to the poet's audience—the fight of Ingeld and Hrothgar. Our knowledge of the story is derived chiefly from the *Widsith* (see lines 45 ff.), which is the only other Old English poem that contains mention of the more important characters of the *Beowulf*.

a noble scion of the Danes,[1] for on him gleam the heir-
looms of their fathers, hard and ring-adorned, once the
Heathobards' treasure, while they could still wield their
weapons, until in an evil day they led astray into battle
their dear companions and their own lives.

"Then speaks one over the beer, an old warrior who
sees the heirloom and who remembers all the slaughter
of the men; and his soul is wrathful; and, sore at heart,
he begins to try the spirit of the young warrior by the
thoughts of his breast, begins to waken war-fury, and
speaks this word: 'Knowst thou the sword, my friend, the
precious blade that thy father bore into battle, when he
wore his helmet for the last time, and the Danes, the bold
Scyldings, slew him, and held the battle-field, because
Withergild [2] was laid low after the fall of heroes? Now
some stripling, offspring of those murderers, walks our
hall exulting in the spoil, boasts of that slaughter, and
wears the treasure which thou shouldst rightly have.'

"Thus he ever goads him and stirs his memory with
galling words, until the hour comes that the lady's [3] thane,
because of his father's deeds, sleeps in blood after the
sword-stroke, forfeiting his life; but the other escapes
thence alive, for well he knows the land. Thus the warrior's oaths on both sides are broken, for deadly hate wells
up in Ingeld's heart, and the love of the woman grows
cooler within him, because of overwhelming woe.

"Therefore I count not sincere the faith of the Heatho-

[1] Heathobards, that is, are obliged to serve some Dane
who has come in attendance on Freawaru.
[2] Nothing is known of him.
[3] Freawaru's.

bards nor their part in the peace with the Danes, nor do I count their friendship firm."

"I must say on and tell again of Grendel, that thou mayst fully know, O king, to what issue the grappling came. After the jewel of heaven had glided over earth, the furious monster, the dread night-foe, came to find us out, where we all unharmed were watching over the hall. There slaughter and an awful death befell Hondscio,[1] for he was doomed; that girded warrior was the first to fall, for Grendel bit him and slew him, our great kinsman-thane; he devoured the whole body of the man we loved. Yet none the sooner would the bloody-toothed murderer, bent on destruction, get him from the hall with empty hands. But he made trial of me and seized upon me with his ready claw. His pouch, wondrous and large, was hanging, fast in cunning bonds; it was all curiously wrought with dragon-skins and strange device of fiends. The bold ill-doer thought to put me therein, me, all sinless, and many another; but he could not so, when I in wrath arose and stood upright. It is too long to recount how I paid the enemy of that people a reward for his every crime. There, O my lord, did I bring glory to thy people by my

[1] See page 41.

deeds. He escaped and fled away—a little while he enjoyed the delights of life; but his right arm he left in Heorot, marking his track, and humbled, in woeful mood, fell thence to the bottom of the mere.

"When morning was come and we had sat down to the feast, the lord of the Scyldings richly rewarded me for that great fight, with beaten gold and many a treasure. There was song and glee. The aged Scylding, when he had asked of many things, told of the days of yore. At times a brave warrior touched the joyous harp, that instrument of mirth; at times he told a tale, truthful and sad; at times the great-hearted king would relate aright some strange legend; at times the hoary warrior, stricken with age, would lament his youth and battle-strength; his heart swelled within him as, old in winters, he thought on all the number of his days.

"So all day long we took our pleasure there, until another night came unto men. And straight thereafter, Grendel's mother was ready for vengeance; sorrowful she journeyed, for death and the war-wrath of the Geats had taken her son. The she-monster avenged her child. Furiously she slew a warrior. Life went from Æschere, the agèd counsellor. Nor could the Danes, when morning was come, burn the corpse with fire, nor lay the belovèd man upon the funeral pile, for in her fiendish clutch she had borne away the body beneath the mountain stream. That was the bitterest of all the griefs that had long befallen Hrothgar, prince of the people. Then the king, heavy-hearted, besought me by thy life to do a hero's deed, to venture my life and win glory in the rush of waters; he promised me reward.

"Then, as is well known, I found the grim and awful guardian of the deep. And there we fought for a time, hand to hand; the mere was welling with gore. With a mighty sword I smote off the head of Grendel's mother in that sea-hall. Hardly did I get thence with my life, but not yet was I doomed. Thereafter the son of Healfdene, defence of warriors, gave me many treasures.

XXXI [1]

Beowulf makes an end of his story, and giveth Hygelac all the gifts which he had of Hrothgar. Hygelac rewardeth him again.

"So the king of that people lived in seemly wise. I lost not my reward, the meed of valor, for the son of Healfdene gave me gifts to use at mine own will, which I will bring and gladly offer thee, O hero-king. Every good thing comes from thee, and I have few blood-kinsmen saving thee, O Hygelac."

And he bade them bring in the boar head-crest, the helm towering in battle, the gray byrnie, and the splendid war-sword, and thereupon he uttered these words: "Hrothgar, the wise prince, gave me this battle-armor, bidding me with express words to give thee first his kindly greeting; and he said that King Heorogar,[2] lord of the Scyldings, long possessed it, nevertheless he would not give the breast-mail to his own son, bold Heoroward, gracious though he was to him. Do thou enjoy it well."

[1] The numbers XXIX and XXX are wanting in the MS., but no part of the text is lost.

[2] Hrothgar's own brother; see page 12.

I have learned that four dappled horses, all alike, followed upon the gift of the armor; graciously he presented unto him the horses and the treasures. So should a kinsman do, and nowise weave a cunning snare for his fellow, and plot the death of his comrade with secret craft. Full loyal was that nephew to Hygelac, the battle-strong; each took thought for the other's joy.

I have heard that he gave to Hygd the necklace, the wondrous jewel curiously wrought, which Wealhtheow, a king's daughter, had given him, and three horses therewith, slender and brightly saddled. Thereafter was her breast adorned, even from the time when she received the circlet.

Thus the son of Ecgtheow behaved himself in glorious wise, he who was famed for his warfare and for his gracious deeds; full honorably he lived, nor did he slay his hearth-companions when they were drunken;[1] his heart was not cruel, but the brave warrior with the greatest care of all mankind held fast the bounteous gift which God had given him.

Long had he been despised,[2] so that the sons of

[1] This strange praise may be contrasted with the criticism of the evil Heremod, page 81.

[2] His youth, like that of Brutus, had given no promise of his later glory.

the Geats had esteemed him not, nor would the
leader of the war-hosts do him much honor at the
mead-bench; oft had they deemed him slothful, an
unwarlike prince. That glorious man was rewarded for his every sorrow.

Then the king, the defence of heroes, strong in
battle, bade them bring in the heirloom of Hrethel,
all decked with gold,—there was no dearer sword
among the treasures of the Geats.[1]   He laid it in
Beowulf's lap; and he gave to him seven thousand
pieces of money, and a hall and a princely seat.
The twain, by right of birth, held land in the
nation, a home and its rights, but Hygelac had
the broad kingdom, and therein he was the greater
man.[2]

[1] Beowulf already possessed his coat of mail; see page 29.
[2] The implication is merely that Beowulf is now the
second man in the nation.

Part III

BEOWULF AND THE DRAGON

XXXI—*Continued*

How Beowulf became king and reigned for fifty years, and how a great Dragon, who watched over a vast treasure-hoard, wasted his land.

THEREAFTER in later days by reason of the crash of battle it fell thus; after Hygelac was laid low,[1] and Heardred had been slain by war-swords piercing beneath the shield, at the time when the War-Scylfings, fierce battle-wolves, fell upon him among his victorious people and overwhelmed the nephew of Hereric in war—after that, the broad kingdom came into the hand of Beowulf. He ruled it well for fifty winters—and the king, aged guardian of the land, was old—until a certain dragon began to hold sway on dark nights and work his

[1] Hygelac was slain in the raid mentioned above, page 60, note 3. His son, Heardred, the "nephew of Hereric," ruled for a short time (see p. 109) until he was attacked by the War-Scylfings (Swedes), and slain in the ensuing battle.

will, one who on a high mound [1] kept watch over
a treasure-hoard in a steep and rocky cave. Beneath it lay a path, unknown to men.

But a certain slave entered there and eagerly
took from the heathen hoard; [2] he seized with his
hand a cup, bright with gold. Nor did he give
it back, albeit he had beguiled the keeper of the
hoard with thievish craft. The king, best of
heroes, learned of that deed, and he was filled with
wrath.

XXXII

Of the hoard in the mound and how the Dragon came by it.
The wrath of the Dragon.

NOWISE of his own freewill and purpose did the
slave seek out the dragon's hoard, and bring sore
harm upon himself, but in dire need, this thrall
of one among the children of men had fled from
wrathful blows, a homeless wretch, haunted by
sin, and he had entered there. But soon it had
come to pass that awful terror seized upon the in-

---

[1] The poet is thinking of a barrow, or burial mound.
[2] At this point the MS. is sadly mutilated. Six lines
are only partially legible. Bugge's reconstruction of them
is used, except for the word king, which is from Morris-
Wyatt.

vader;[1] . . . just as the terror got hold of him he saw the precious cup.

Many olden treasures were lying in that cave of earth where a certain man in days of yore had hidden away the dear possessions, taking thought for the great bequest of his noble kin. Death had snatched away those men in times gone by, and, at the last, the one who tarried longest there of all that mighty line was mourning for his friends; yet he would fain live that he might enjoy for a little time those olden treasures.

There was a new mound ready on the plain, near to the cliff hard by the ocean-waves, made fast by cunning craft. Thither the keeper of rings bore that heavy store of beaten gold, the princely treasures; and he spoke a few words: "Now do thou hold, O Earth—since heroes could not hold —this princely treasure, for, lo! in thee at first the good men found it. Every man of my people who hath yielded up this life, dread slaughter, death in war, hath swept away—they had known the pleasures of the hall. None have I to wield the sword, none to burnish the plated beaker, the precious drinking-cup—the warrior-heroes are departed otherwhere. The hard helmet, decked with gold,

[1] Three illegible lines.

must be reft of its adornments; they sleep who once did brighten it, they who prepared the masks of war. Likewise the coat of mail which, amid the crash of shields, was proof against the bite of swords in battle, moulders with the hero; the byrnie may no longer make far journeys with the warleader, together with heroes. There is no joy of harp, no mirth of the gleewood, no good hawk swinging through the hall, no swift horse beating with his hoof the courts about the hall. Baleful death hath sent forth many mortals on their way." Thus, alone and heavy-hearted, he sorrowfully lamented for them all, mournfully weeping by day and night until the surge of death touched at his heart.

Then the beauteous hoard, standing all open, had been found by the old twilight foe, the naked venomous [1] dragon, he who, wrapped in flames, haunteth the mounds, and flies by night begirt with fire; of him the dwellers in the land are sore afraid. It is his wont to find out some hoard in the earth, where, old in winters, he may guard the heathen gold—but naught the better will he fare for that.

Thus for three hundred winters the scourge of

---

[1] The old conception of serpent-guarded treasure is found in Kipling's *King's Ankus*.

the people had held the vast treasure-cave within the earth, until a certain man [1] angered him in his heart, and bore away the plated beaker to his lord, and prayed his master for a covenant of peace. Thus the hoard was plundered, and a part of the treasure taken away. But his boon was granted to that wretched man. His lord beheld for the first time that handiwork of ancient men.

Soon as the dragon woke, strife was begun; fierce at heart he sniffed along the rock, and found out the tracks of his foe, for with secret craft he had gone on too far, hard by the dragon's head. So the man not doomed to die easily escapeth woe and banishment, even he whom the grace of the Lord upholdeth. The keeper of the hoard sought eagerly along the ground, he wished to find the man who had wrought him this mischief in his sleep. Wroth and hot-hearted, he circled oft about the mound without—but there was none upon the waste. Yet he rejoiced in the thought of battle, in warfare to come. At times he would turn back to the mound, and seek his precious cup. Soon he was ware that some one of menfolk had found out the gold, his splendid treasure.

Impatiently the keeper of the hoard waited till

[1] The slave.

even was come; the guardian of the mound was mad with wrath; the foe wished to repay them with fire and burning for the loss of his dear cup. And the day departed, even as the dragon wished. No longer, then, would he abide in his den, but went forth flaming, all girdled with fire. Fearful was the beginning for the men of that land, even as the end was bitter, which straight thereafter fell upon their gracious lord.

XXXIII

The Dragon burneth Beowulf's hall, and the old king maketh
ready to go out against him. Of Beowulf's early deeds
in battle, and of the death of Heardred.

THEN the monster began to spew forth coals of fire and burn the bright dwellings; the surging flame leaped forth, affrighting the people; the loathèd flier of the air meant to leave naught in that place alive. The warfare of the dragon, the vengeance of the deadly foe, near and far was manifest, how the destroyer hated and humbled the Geatish folk. Ere break of day he shot back to his hoard again, to his dark and secret hall. He had compassed the men of that land with flame, with fire and burning, trusting for defence in his mound, his wall, and his might in warfare. Vain was that trust.

And forthwith the terror was made known to Beowulf, how for a truth his own home, best of halls, the gift-seat of the Geats, had melted away in waves of fire. The good man suffered pain at heart, most grievous sorrow; the wise hero thought that, sinning against the ancient laws, he had provoked to anger the Almighty, the Lord eternal; his breast within him surged with dark thoughts, as was not his wont.

The fire-dragon with his burning coals had utterly destroyed the fortress, stronghold of the people, the water-washed fastness. Therefore the war-king, chief of the Weders, devised revenge upon him. Then the defence of warriors, lord of heroes, bade them make him a wondrous battle-shield, all of iron; for he knew full well that a shield of linden wood from the forest could avail him naught against the flame. But the valiant prince was doomed to meet the end of his fleeting days, of this worldly life, and the dragon too, though he had long held the hoarded treasure.

But the ring-prince scorned to seek out the wide-flying pest with a host of men, a great army; he had no fear of the combat for himself, nor did he es-

teem at all the dragon's war-might, his strength
and prowess; forasmuch as aforetime, though in
narrow straits, he had come safe through many a
contest, many a battle-crash, since the time when,
crowned with victory, he cleansed Hrothgar's
hall, and closed in fight with Grendel's kin of
loathèd race.

Nor was that the least of contests[1] in which
Hygelac, son of Hrethel, was slain in the storm of
battle, when the king of the Geats, kind lord of the
people, was smitten by the blade, and the sword
drank his life in Friesland. Thence Beowulf
came off by his own strength, swimming the waves;
upon his arm he had thirty suits of armor, when
all alone he went down to the sea. The Hetwaras,[2]
who had borne out their shields against him, had
no cause to boast of their warfare, for few escaped
from that war-wolf unto their home. So the son
of Ecgtheow, wretched and alone, swam over the
expanse of the waters back to his own people.
There Hygd offered him the kingdom and the
treasure, wealth and royal throne, for she put no
trust in her child, that he would be able to hold the

[1] At this point the poet chooses to pause and tell us
how Beowulf had come to the throne. Cf. page 102.

[2] The tribe against whom Hygelac's expedition was
directed.

native seats against foreign tribes, now that Hygelac was dead. Yet none the sooner could the
bereaved people persuade the prince on any condi-
tions to become Heardred's lord and take the kingdom; but rather did he uphold Heardred among
the people with friendly counsel, with favor, and
with honor, until he grew older and ruled the
Weder-Geats.

But banished men, the sons of Ohthere,[1] came
to his land from overseas; they had rebelled against
the lord of the Scylfings, the great prince, best of
the sea-kings that dealt out treasure in the Swedish
land. Hence came Heardred's end; Hygelac's son,
for that he harbored them, got his death from
sword-blows. And, after the fall of Heardred,
the son of Ongentheow returned to his home, and
suffered Beowulf to have the royal throne, and rule
over the Geats—he was a good king.

[1] Heardred harbors two Swedish outlaws, much as
Hrothgar had harbored Beowulf's father long before
(pages 29–30). The Swedish general, the "son of Ongentheow," pursues them, and a battle between the two nations
ensues in which Heardred is killed.

XXXIV

How Heardred was avenged. Beowulf goes forth. He tells
of his early years and of the death of Herebeald and
Haethcyn, and now Hygelac was king.

In later days Beowulf bethought him of retribution for the prince's [1] fall; he befriended the
wretched Eadgils. Sailing over the broad sea, he
supported the son of Ohthere with his army, with
his warriors and weapons. Thereafter Eadgils
avenged himself for his drear and bitter exile, and
took the life of the king.[2]

Thus the son of Ecgtheow had come safe through
his every conflict, every perilous fight and brave
adventure, even unto that great day in which he
was to give battle to the dragon. Then the lord of
the Geats, being filled with wrath, went forth with
eleven companions to look upon the serpent. He
had learned how the feud arose, and all the mischief to his men, for he had received the goodly
treasure-cup from the hand of him who found it.
He was the thirteenth in the band, even the man
who had caused the beginning of the feud, a captive
sad at heart. Him they compelled in downcast

[1] Heardred's.   [2] Ongentheow.

III

mood to guide them to the spot. Unwillingly he went to where he knew that earth-hall stood, a cavern under ground, hard by the struggling waves and the surge of waters; within, it was full of jewels and twisted gold. The awful guardian, a ready fighter, had long watched his golden treasures under earth. No easy task was it for any man to purchase entrance there.

Then the king, strong in battle, the bounteous lord of the Geats, sat him down upon the headland, while he bade farewell to his hearth-companions. His spirit was full of sorrow, wavering, and ready to depart; Wyrd was upon him, she who was to come unto that aged man, to seek out the treasure of his soul and put asunder body and life; no long time was it now that the prince's soul was to be wrapped in flesh. Beowulf, son of Ecgtheow, spoke: "In my youth I passed through many a battle-onset, many an hour of strife; I remember all. I was seven winters old when the treasure-prince, dear lord of the people, received me at my father's hand; King Hrethel [1] had me and held me as his own; he gave me of his treasure and his food, remembering our kinship. Never, while a thane in his hall, was I a whit less dear to him than any

[1] His grandfather, Hygelac's father.

of his sons, Herebeald, Hæthcyn, or Hygelac my lord.
For the eldest born a kinsman's deed did strew the
bed of death, as was not meet, for Hæthcyn laid him
low, him his dear lord, with a bolt from his bow
of horn; he missed the mark, and shot his kinsman
down—with bloody dart brother did brother slay.
It was a deed sinfully committed, not to be atoned,[1]
sickening to the heart, yet howe'er it were, the prince
must needs depart from life unavenged.

"In like manner it is a piteous thing for an
aged man to live to see his young son swinging
upon the gallows; he utters his lament, his song
of woe, while his son hangeth there for the raven's
delight, and he, old and full of years, can do
naught to help him. Ever at morn is he minded
of his son's departure, cares to await another heir
within his home, since this one, through the pangs
of death, hath received for his deeds. Worn with
sorrow, he seeth in his son's dwelling, all bereft
of revelry, a deserted wine-hall, where the winds
linger—riders and heroes are sleeping in the
grave; there is no sound of harp, no joy within the
courts, as formerly there was."

[1] The close family relationship forbids the natural de-
mand for vengeance and weregild. In the next paragraph
Beowulf imagines a somewhat similar case, in which a
father cannot take vengeance for his dead son.

XXXV

Beowulf ends his discourse, and bids farewell to his thanes.
He shouts aloud, and the Dragon comes forth. The
fight begins. It goes hard with Beowulf.

"Then he goes to his bed, chanting in his lone-
liness a lamentation for the departed one; fields
and dwelling-place, all seem too large for him.
Even so suffered the defence of the Weders,[1] while
his heart surged with sorrow in memory of Herebeald. In nowise could he avenge the feud upon
the murderer; none the sooner with hostile deeds
could he wreak his hatred on the warrior, though
he was not dear to him. Then, because of the
sorrow which that wound cost him, he gave o'er
the joys of men and chose the light of God. He
left to his sons, as a rich man is wont, his land and
his cities, when he departed from life.

"Then, after Hrethel's death, there was feud
and strife, war and struggle fierce between the
Geats and the Swedes over the wide water; and
the sons of Ongentheow grew bold and eager for
warfare;[2] they would not keep the peace beyond

[1] Hrethel.
[2] The paragraph becomes clearer if compared with
another later account, pages 132 ff.

the seas, but made many a fierce raid about Hreosnabeorh. For that my kinsmen took revenge, for
the feud and the treachery, as was well known,
although one bought it with his life—a heavy price;
Hæthcyn, lord of the Geats, fell in that war. But
I heard men say that in the morning, when Ongentheow met with Eofor, brother avenged brother
upon the murderer, with the edge of the sword;
the helmet was split asunder—Ongentheow, the
aged Scylfing, fell, pale in death; the hand that
smote remembered feuds enough, it did not with-
hold the death-blow.

"Then in my warfare it was granted me to pay
Hygelac with my flashing sword for the treasures
he had given me. He bestowed upon me land,
a dwelling-place and the joys of a home. He did
not need to seek out a worse warrior among the
Gifths or the Spear-Danes or in the Swedish realm,
and hire him for pay. Ever was I wont to be before him in his host, alone in the van. And even
so all my life long will I wage warfare, while lasts
this sword which has often served me early and
late, ever since in my valor I slew Dæghrefn with
my hand, him who was champion of the Hugas.
By no means was he suffered to carry spoils, fair
breast-adornments, to the Frisian king, for the

standard-keeper fell in battle, a prince in his might; he was not slain with the sword—the grapple of war crushed his body and the beating of his heart. But now the edge of the sword, hand and hard blade, must do battle for the treasure."

Beowulf spoke; for the last time he uttered boastful words: "In the days of my youth I ventured on many battles; and even now will I, aged guardian of my people, go into fight and do memorable deeds, if the great destroyer come forth to me out of his den." Then for the last time he greeted each of the men, bold helmet-wearers, his own dear companions. "I would not bear a sword or any weapon against the Serpent, if I knew how else I could make good my boast against the monster, as I did of old against Grendel. But I look for hot battle-fire there, for the venomous blast of his nostrils; therefore I have upon me shield and byrnie. I will not flee one foot's breadth from the keeper of that mound, but it shall be with us twain at the wall as Wyrd, lord of every man, allotteth. I am eager in spirit, so that I forbear boasting against the wingèd warrior. But do ye men tarry upon the mound with your armor upon you, clad in your byrnies, to see which of us twain after the strife shall survive the deadly woundings.

It is no exploit for you, nor for the might of any man, save mine alone to measure strength with the monster and do a hero's deeds. I will boldly win the gold, or else battle, yea an evil death, shall take away your lord."

Then the mighty warrior rose up with his shield, stern under his helmet; he bore his battle-mail beneath the stony cliffs. He trusted in his single strength. That is no coward's way. And he beheld hard by the wall—he of noble worth, who had passed through many wars and clashing battles when armed hosts close in fight—where stood an arch of stone and a stream breaking out thence from the mound; the surge of the stream was hot with fire. The hero could not anywhile endure unburned the hollow nigh the hoard, because of the dragon's flame.

Then the lord of the Geats, for he was wroth, sent forth a word from his breast. The stout-hearted warrior stormed; his voice, battle-clear, entered in and rang under the hoary rock. The keeper of the hoard knew the speech of men, and his hate was stirred. No further chance was there for peace. First came forth out of the rock the breath of the evil beast, the hot reek of battle. The earth resounded. The hero beneath the mound, lord of the Geats, swung up his shield against the awful foe, and the heart of the coiled monster waxed eager for the strife. Already the good warrior-king had drawn his sword, that olden heirloom, undulled of edge. Either destroyer struck awe in the other. But stout-hearted stood that prince of friends against his tall shield, while the dragon coiled himself quickly together; the armed man waited.

Then the flaming dragon, curving like a bow, advanced upon him, hastening to his fate. A shorter time the shield warded the life and body of the mighty king than his hopes had looked for, if haply he were to prevail in the combat at that time, early in the day; but Wyrd did not thus allot. The lord of the Geats lifted his hand and smote the hideous-gleaming foe with his weighty sword, in such wise that the brown blade weakened as it fell upon the bone, and bit less deeply than its lord had need, when sore beset. Then, at the sword-stroke, the keeper of the mound raged furiously. He cast forth devouring fire. Far and wide shot deadly flame. The lord of the Geats nowise boasted of victory, for his naked war-sword, that good blade, weakened in the fight, as was not meet. It was no easy course for the

mighty son of Ecgtheow to forsake this earth for
ever; yet he was doomed against his will to take
up his abode in a dwelling otherwhere. So every
man must quit these fleeting days.

It was not long ere the fighters closed again.
The keeper of the hoard plucked up his courage;
his breast heaved anew with his venomous breath-
ing. He who erewhile ruled the people was hard
put to it, being compassed with fire. In nowise
did his own companions, sons of heroes, surround
him in a band with warlike valor, but they took
refuge in the wood to save their lives. There was
but one among them whose heart surged with sorrows. Naught can ever put aside the bond of
kinship in him who thinketh aright.

XXXVI

*Wiglaf, a young thane of Beowulf's, upbraids his fellows
and goes to the help of the old king. Beowulf's sword
is shattered in the fight, and he gets a deadly wound.*

He was called Wiglaf, son of Weohstan, a beloved warrior, lord of the Scylfings, kinsman of
Ælfhere. He saw his lord suffering the heat under
his helmet; and he was minded of all the benefits
which Beowulf had given him in time past, the rich

dwelling-place of the Wægmundings, and every folk-right which his father possessed. And he could not forbear, but seized the shield, the yellow linden, with his hand, and drew forth his old sword. This was known among men as an heirloom of Eanmund, son of Ohthere, whom, when a friend-less exile, Weohstan slew in fight with the edge of the sword; he bore to his kinsman the brown hel-met, the ringèd byrnie, the old giant-sword that Onela had given him; they were his comrade's war-harness, his ready armor. He spoke not of the feud, though he had killed his brother's son. He held the spoils, the sword and byrnie, for many years until his son could do a hero's deeds, like his father before him. Then he gave to him, among the Geats, all manner of armors, when, full of years, he passed hence from life.

This was the first time that the young warrior was to partake in the storm of war with his high lord. But his heart melted not within him, nor did his kinsman's heirloom weaken in the fight. That the dragon learned when they were come together.

Wiglaf spoke many fitting words, saying to his companions—for his soul was sad within him:—"I remember the time when, as we drank the mead in hall, we promised our lord, him who gave us these rings, that we would repay him for the war-harness, for helmet and hard sword, if need like this befell him. Of his own will he chose us from his host for this adventure, urged us to do gloriously, and gave me these treasures, since he deemed us good spearmen, keen helm-bearers; albeit our lord, defender of his people, had thought to do this mighty work alone, for that he of all men hath performed most of famed exploits and daring deeds. Now the day is come when our lord needs the might of good warriors. Let us on to his help, whilst the heat is upon him, and the grim terror of fire.

"God knows of me that I would much rather that the flame enwrap my body with my king's. Methinks it unseemly that we should bear our shields back to our home, unless we can first strike down the foe and defend the life of the Weders' king. Full well I know that it is not according to his old deserts that he alone of all the Geatish force should suffer pain and sink in fight. We twain will have one sword and one helmet, one shield and one byrnie in common."

Then with his war-helmet he sped through the noisome smoke, to the aid of his lord; he spoke a few words: "Belovèd Beowulf, now do thou all

things well, as thou of old sworest in the days of thy
youth that thou wouldst not let thy glory wane
while thou didst live. Now, O stedfast hero, famed
for thy deeds, do thou defend thy life with all thy
might. Lo, I will help thee."

After these words, the dragon, awful monster,
flashing with blazing flames, came on all wroth
a second time to meet his hated foes. Wiglaf's
shield was burned away to the boss in the waves
of fire; the byrnie could give no help to the young
spear-warrior. But the youth went quickly under
his kinsman's shield, since his own had been burned
to ashes by the flames. Then again the war-king
took thought for his glory; mightily he smote with
his battle-sword driving fiercely so that it stood in
the dragon's head. Nægling [1] was shivered in
pieces; Beowulf's sword, old and gray-marked,
weakened in the fight—it was not granted that
the iron blade should help him in the strife. Too
strong was the hand, as I have heard, which by its
blow o'ertaxed all swords whatsoever; so that he
fared none the better for it, when he bore into the
fight a weapon wondrous hard. [2]

---

[1] The name of the sword. Its gray markings are
probably etchings on hilt and blade; cf. page 80.

[2] So mighty is his blow that no sword is strong enough
for him.

Then the destroyer of people, the dread fire-dragon, for the third time was mindful of the feud. He rushed on the brave hero, when ground was yielded him. Hot and fierce, he seized upon Beowulf's whole neck with his sharp teeth. He was all wetted with his life-blood; the gore welled forth in streams.

XXXVII

They slay the Dragon. The king is nigh unto death.

THEN I have heard men tell how, in the king's great need, Wiglaf, the hero, showed forth unceasing courage, skill and valor, as was his nature; he heeded not the dragon's head (though the hero's hand was burned as he helped his kinsman), but the armed man smote the evil beast a little lower down, insomuch that the bright and plated sword drove into him, and the fire began to wane forthwith. Then the king recovered himself; he drew the short-sword, keen and sharp in battle, which he wore on his byrnie. The defence of the Weders cut the Serpent asunder in the middle. They struck down the foe; their might drove forth his life, and thus they twain, noble kinsmen, destroyed him. Even such should a man be, a thane good at need. That was the king's last hour of victory by his own great deeds, the last of his worldly work.

But the wound which the earth-dragon had given him began to burn and swell; presently he found that poison, deadly venom, was surging in his breast. Then the prince, still wise in mind, moved along so that he might seat him by the mound; he saw that work of giants, saw how the rocky arches standing firm on their pillars, upheld within the earth-hall everlasting. Then the thane, surpassing good, taking water, with his hands bathed the great king, his own dear lord, all gory and wearied with battle, and loosed his helm.

Beowulf spoke and uttered words, despite his wound, his piteous battle-hurt; full well he knew that his life of earthly joy was spent, that the appointed number of his days was run, and Death exceeding near: "Now would I give my armor to my son, had I been granted any heir, born of my body, to come after me. Fifty winters have I ruled this people; yet there was never a king of all the neighbor tribes who durst attack me with the sword or threaten me with evil. In my home I awaited what the times held in store for me, kept well mine own, sought out no wily quarrels, swore not many a false oath. In all this I can rejoice, though death-sick with my wounds, inasmuch as the Ruler of men cannot charge me with murder of kinsmen, when my life parteth from my body. Now do thou, dear Wiglaf, lightly go and view the hoard under the gray rock, now the dragon lieth low, sleepeth sore wounded, bereft of his treasure. Do thou make haste that I may behold the olden treasures, that store of gold, and gladly gaze upon those bright and curious gems; and thus, having seen the treasured wealth, I may the easier quit life and the kingdom which long I have ruled."

XXXVIII

Beowulf beholdeth the treasure, and passeth.

And I have heard how the son of Weohstan, after these words, quickly obeyed his wounded lord, sick from the battle; he bore his ringèd mail-shirt, the woven battle-sark, under the roof of the cave. And the brave thane, exultant victor, as he went by the seat, saw many precious jewels, much glistering gold lying upon the ground and wondrous treasures on the wall, and the den of the dragon, the old twilight-flier; bowls lay there, vessels of bygone men, with none to brighten them, their adornments fallen away. There was many

125

a helmet old and rusty, many an arm-ring cunningly twisted. Treasure of gold found in the earth can easily puff with pride the heart of any man, hide it who will. Likewise he saw a banner all of gold standing there, high above the hoard, greatest of wonders, woven by skill of hand; from it there shone a ray of light, so that he could see the cavern floor, and examine the fair jewels. Naught was to be seen of the dragon there, for the sword had undone him.

Thus I have heard how one man alone at his own free will plundered the hoard within the cave, the old work of the giants, how he laid in his bosom beakers and dishes; he took the banner, too, that brightest of beacons. The old lord's blade, with its iron edge, had sorely injured him who long had been the owner of these treasures, who at midnight had borne about the fiery terror, dreadfully surging, hot before the hoard, until he died the death.

The messenger was in haste, eager to return, urged by thought of his spoil. The great-hearted man was spurred with longing to know whether he would find alive the lord of the Weders, grievously sick, in the place where he had left him. And bringing the treasures, he found the great

prince, his lord, bleeding, at the point of death;
he began to sprinkle him again with water until
the word's point broke through the treasure of his
heart, and Beowulf spoke, aged and sorrowful, as
he gazed upon the gold: "I utter thanks unto the
Ruler of all, King of Glory, everlasting Lord, for
these fair things, which here I look upon, inasmuch as ere my death-day I have been able to
win them for my people. I have sold and paid
mine aged life for the treasure-hoard. Fulfil ye
now the needs of the people.[1]   Here can I be no
more. Bid the brave warriors rear a splendid
mound at the sea-cape after my body is burned.
There on Whale's Ness shall it tower high as a
memorial for my people, so that seafarers, they
who drive from far their great ships over the misty
floods, may in aftertime call it 'Beowulf's Mound.'"

The great-hearted king took from his neck the
ring of gold; gave to his thane, the youthful warrior, his helmet gold-adorned, his ring and his
byrnie, bade him enjoy them well.

"Thou art the latest left of all our kin, the
Wægmundings. Wyrd hath swept away all my
kinsmen, heroes in their might, to the appointed
doom. I must after them."

[1] Cf. the whole scene with Layamon's *Brut*, ll. 14291 ff.

That was the old king's last word from the thoughts of his heart, ere he yielded to the bale-fire and the hotly surging flames. His soul departed from out his bosom unto the reward of the righteous.

XXXIX

Wiglaf bitterly upbraids those craven thanes.

Thus it went full hard with the young man to see his best-beloved one lying lifeless on the ground, faring most wretchedly. His destroyer lay there too, the horrid earth-dragon, bereft of life, crushed in ruin. No longer could the coiled serpent rule over treasure-hoards, for the edge of the sword, the hard, battle-notched work of the hammer, had destroyed him, and he had fallen to the ground near his hoard-hall, stilled by the wounding. No more in play did he whirl through the air at midnight, and show himself forth, proud of his treasure, for he sank to earth by the mighty hand of the battle-chief.

Indeed, as I have heard, it hath prospered few men in the world, even though mighty, however daring in their every deed, to rush on against the blasts of a venomous foe, or to meddle with his

treasure-house, if haply they found the keeper
waking, abiding in his mound. Beowulf paid with
his death for his share in the lordly wealth. Both
of them had reached the end of this fleeting life.

It was not long thereafter that the cowards left
the wood, those craven traitors, the ten of them
together, even they who in their lord's great need
had not dared to brandish spear. But shamefully
now they bore their shields, their war-armor, to
where the old man lay. They looked upon Wiglaf. The wearied warrior was sitting by his lord's
shoulder; he was trying to revive him with water,
but it availed him naught. He could not stay the
chieftain's life on earth, though dearly he wished
it, nor change the will of God in aught. The judgment of the Lord was wont to rule the deeds of
every man, even as it doth to-day.

And straightway the youth had a fierce and
ready answer for those whose courage had failed
them.[1] Wiglaf, son of Weohstan, spoke, sad at
heart, as he looked upon those hated men: "Lo!
he who is minded to speak the truth may say that
the liege lord, he who gave you these treasures, even
the battle-armor in which ye are standing—what
time at the ale-bench the king gave oft unto his

[1] Cf. *Germania* 14; the *Battle of Maldon*, ll. 245 ff.

thanes, sitting in the hall, helms and byrnies, the
choicest far or near which he could find—utterly
and wretchedly wasted that war-harness.   Nowise
did the king need to boast of his comrades in arms
when strife overtook him; yet God, the Lord of
victory, granted him unaided to avenge him with
the sword, when he had need of valor.   Little protection could I give him in the fight; and yet I
tried what was beyond my power—to help my kinsman.   It was ever the worse for the deadly foe
when I smote him with the sword, the fire less
fiercely flamed from his head.   Too few defenders
thronged about their lord when the dread moment
fell.   Now, all sharing of treasure, all gift of
swords, all hope, all rights of home, shall cease
from your kin.   Every man of your house shall
roam, bereft of tribal rights, as soon as the princes
in far countries hear of your flight, your inglorious
deed.   Death [1] is better for every man than a life
of shame!"

[1] Banishment, unless other "tribal rights" might be
obtained elsewhere, was little better than death.

XL AND XLI

Beowulf's death is announced to the host. The messenger discourses. The people go to the place of the fight.

THEN he bade announce the issue of the fight to the stronghold up over the sea-cliff, where the sad warrior-band had been sitting by their shields the morning long, looking for either the death or the return of their dear lord.   Little did he keep silence of the new tidings, he who rode up the headland, but truthfully spoke before them all: "Now the chief of the Weder people, lord of the Geats, source of all our joy, is fast in the bed of death; he lieth low in slaughter because of the Dragon's deeds. Beside him lieth his deadly foe, slain by the wounding of the knife; for with the sword he could nowise wound the monster. Wiglaf, son of Weohstan, sitteth over Beowulf, the living hero by the dead; over his head with weary heart he keepeth watch or friend and foe.[1]

"Now the nation may look for a season of war as soon as the fall of the king is published abroad among Franks and Frisians. A fierce strife with

[1] Death-watch for Beowulf and for the Dragon.

the Hugas arose [1] when Hygelac came with a ship-army into Frisian land; there the Hetwaras vanquished him in battle; by their valor, with an overwhelming army, they forced the mailed warrior to sink in the fight; he fell amid his host. The prince gave no spoils to his warriors. Ne'er since then has the favor of the Merovingian [2] been granted us.

THE BATTLE OF RAVENSWOOD

The messenger telleth how Ongentheow, king of the Swedes, besieged the Geats in Ravenswood until King Hygelac came to them. How two Geatish brothers, Eofor and Wulf, killed King Ongentheow in the battle that followed, and how they were rewarded by Hygelac.

"Nor do I anywise look for peace or truth from the Swedes,[3] for it was widely known that Ongentheow took the life of Hæthcyn, son of Hrethel, near Ravenswood, what time the War-Scylfings in vainglory did first attack the Geats. Straightway the aged father of Ohthere, old

---

[1] See pages 60, 109.
[2] A second authentic historical allusion. The supremacy of the Merovingians lasted until 752. It is obvious that this part of the poem was in existence before that date.
[3] The messenger in forecasting the renewed enmity of the Swedes as one of the national results of Beowulf's death, recalls an ancient feud with them which illustrates their hostility.

and terrible, returned the blow; he slew Hæthcyn, the sea-
king, the old man rescued his wife, though robbed of her
gold, his spouse, mother of Ohthere and Onela, and then
he followed after his deadly foes, until they escaped with
pain into Ravenswood, reft of their lord. Then with a
great army he beset the remnant left by the sword, weary
with their wounds; oft during all that night did he threaten
woe to the hapless band; said that on the morrow he
would slay them with the edge of the sword, and hang
some of them on the gallows to delight the birds.

"With daybreak comfort came to the heavy-hearted
men, when they heard Hygelac's horn and the blast of his
trumpet, as the good king came marching on in their track
with his mighty men.

"Far and wide was to be seen the bloody track of
Swedes and Geats, the warriors' deadly strife—how the
peoples, together wakened the feud. Then the good chief
Ongentheow, aged and downcast, fell back with his clansmen to the stronghold, the warrior turned again towards
the upland; he had learned of the proud chief's warfare,
of Hygelac's might in battle. He trusted not in resistance, trusted not that he could defy the seamen, the
ocean-farers, and defend his treasure, his children, and
wife; the old man drew back thence under the earth-wall.

"Then chase was given to the Swedish folk. Forth
went Hygelac's standards over that peace-plain, until
the Hrethlings[1] thronged up to the inclosure. There
Ongentheow, the white-haired, was driven to bay with
the edge of the sword, so that the mighty king was forced
to yield wholly to the will of Eofor. Wulf, son of Wonred,

[1] Hrethel's men, the Geats.

133

struck at him fiercely with his weapon so that at the blow the blood burst forth in streams beneath his hair. Yet the aged Scylfing was not daunted; for the king quickly repaid that deadly stroke with worse exchange, when he turned upon him. The swift son of Wonred could not strike that aged man again, for Ongentheow had cleft the helmet on his head, so that he was forced to bow; stained with blood, he fell to earth. But he was not yet doomed, for he recovered himself again, though the wound had touched him nearly. Then, when his brother had fallen, Hygelac's brave thane [1] let his broad blade, his old giant-sword, break through the wall of shields down into the giant-fashioned helm, and the king, defence of the people, bowed him low, mortally wounded.

"There were many who bound up the wounds of the brother;[2] upraised him quickly when the place was cleared for them, so that they could be masters of the battle-field; meanwhile the one warrior stripped the other—Eofor took from Ongentheow his iron byrnie, his hard and hilted sword, with his helmet, too.

"They bore to Hygelac the old man's war-harness. He received the spoil, and graciously promised them rewards among his people; and he performed it even so. The lord of the Geats, the son of Hrethel, when he had returned home, repaid Eofor and Wulf for their deadly fight with treasure exceeding great; he gave to each of them a hundred thousand in land and twisted rings; nor needed any man on earth reproach him with those rewards, since they had won glory in the fight. And, moreover, as

[1] Eofor who now avenges his brother Wulf by slaying Ongentheow. [2] Wulf.

a pledge of his favor, he gave his only daughter to Eofor in marriage, for an honor to his home.

"Such is the feud and the enmity, men's deadly strife, for which, I ween, the Swedish people will attack us, soon as they learn that our lord is dead, he who upheld our treasure [1] and our realm against the foe, wrought good for his people, and won him, too, a hero's fame.

"Now we had best hasten to look upon our king, and bring our ring-bestower along his way to the pyre. No mean thing shall be burned with the hero, for the hoard of treasure, of untold riches, has been bitterly purchased; and now at the last, he has bought these jewels with his own life. Fire shall devour them, flames shall enwrap them. No warrior shall bear away any of the treasure for a memorial, no fair maiden shall wear upon her neck the jeweled adornment; but rather, bereft of gold and sad at heart, she shall tread the land of the stranger often and often, now that the chieftain has quitted laughter, mirth and glee. Therefore many a spear, cold in the morning, must needs be clasped by the fingers, uplifted in the hand; the sound of the harp shall not waken the warrior, but

[1] An unintelligible line perhaps out of its proper place, "after the fall of heroes, brave Scyldings" is omitted.

the wan raven, eager o'er the doomed, shall chatter freely, telling the eagle [1] how he sped at the feast, when with the wolf he plundered the slain."

Thus the bold hero told his hated tidings: he spoke not falsely touching facts or words. All the band arose; sadly they went, with welling tears, beneath Eagle's Cliff to look upon the marvel. And they found him who had given them treasure in days gone by, found him in his resting-place, lifeless on the sand. Gone was the hero's final day, for the warrior-king, lord of the Weders, had died a wondrous death.

But first they beheld there a stranger being, the loathsome beast lying over against him on the plain; the fiery dragon, awful monster, was all scorched with flames. He was fifty feet long where he lay. At times he had been wont to rejoice in the air in the night season; thereafter down returning to his den. Now he was fast in the clutch of death; he had enjoyed the last of his caverns. By him stood bowls and flagons; dishes lay there, and precious swords, rusty and eaten through, as if they had remained in earth's bosom a thousand winters; for a spell had been wound about that vast

[1] The reference to birds of prey talking of the dead recalls to mind the ballads of *The Two Corbies* and *The Three Ravens.*

heritage, that gold of bygone men, so that none
could touch the treasure-house, save as God himself, the King of victory—He is man's Defence—
should grant unto whom He would, even unto whatsoever man should seem good to Him, to open up
the hoard.

XLII

*The Geats plunder the board and cast the Dragon into
the sea.*

THEN it was manifest that his way did not prosper, who had unrighteously hidden the riches beneath the mound.[1] The guardian had slain some
few of the people and the feud was dreadfully
avenged. It is ever a wonder when a strong hero
reacheth the end of his destined days, then when
he may no longer dwell in hall among his kinsmen.
This was the lot of Beowulf when he went out unto
the guardian of the mound and the deadly strife;
himself he knew not what was to part him from
the world. For the mighty princes, who put the
treasure there, uttered a deep curse upon it to hold
till Doomsday, saying that the men who plundered

---

[1] This seems to be a clumsy reference to the Dragon;
for the context obviously does not allow of our understanding it to be the original owner.

that place should be guilty of sins, imprisoned in idol-fanes, fast bound in the bonds of hell, and visited with plagues. But Beowulf was not greedy for gold; rather had he looked for the grace of the Almighty.[1]

Wiglaf, son of Weohstan, spoke: "Often, for the sake of one man, must many heroes suffer, even as we do now. We could not teach our dear lord, keeper of the realm, any counsel—that he should not go out against the guardian of the gold, but let him lie where long he had been, let him dwell in his haunts till the end of the world. He held to his high fate. The hoard is dearly bought and opened to our view; too cruel was the fate that enticed the king thither. I went within and looked upon all the riches of that cave, for a way had been opened, though not in gentle wise, and a passage granted me in under the earth-wall. Hurriedly I seized with my hands a vast burden of treasure and bore it out hither to my king. And he was yet alive, conscious still and wise of mind. Many things did the aged man speak in his sorrow; and he bade me

---

[1] The whole passage is confused. Two ideas seem to be contaminated, a heathen one and a Christian one: (1) In view of the curse, all who had anything to do with the hoard had suffered; (2) Beowulf's desecration of the hoard was partly in ignorance, and partly in righteous retribution.

138

greet you, prayed that ye would build upon the
place of burning a high mound, great and glorious,
in memory of the deeds of your lord, inasmuch as
he was the worthiest warrior among men over the
broad earth, while he could still enjoy the wealth
of his cities.

"Let us now hasten to go and see the heap of
treasures cunningly wrought, the wonder beneath
the wall; I will guide you that ye may behold and
see, near at hand, abundance of rings and ample
gold. When we come out thence, let the bier be
forthwith made ready, and then let us bear our
master, our beloved lord, to where he shall tarry
long, safe in the keeping of the Almighty."

And the son of Weohstan, the hero bold in battle,
bade that they give command to many warriors,
owners of homes, rulers of men, to bring from far
wood for the pyre to where the good king lay, saying: "Now shall fire consume, while the wan flame
is waxing high, the chief among warriors, him who
oft withstood the shower of darts, what time the
storm of arrows urged by the string flew over the
wall of shields, and the shaft fulfilled its duty, as,
with its feather-fittings, it eagerly sped the barb."

Now the wise son of Weohstan summoned together seven of the king's best thanes from out the

troop, and, himself the eighth, went with them under the hostile roof; one of the warriors, who went at the head, bore in his hand a flaming torch. And when the men had seen some portion of the treasure in the cave, lying there unguarded, and wasting away, in no wise did they choose by lot who should despoil that hoard; and little did it grieve any man among them that the precious treasures were straightway borne out thence.

Moreover, they pushed the Dragon, that serpent, over the sea-cliff, let the wave take him and the waters engulf the keeper of treasure.

There the twisted gold of every sort, past counting, was laden upon a wain. The prince, the hoary warrior, was borne away to Whale's Ness.

XLIII

They burn Beowulf.

THEN the Geatish people fashioned for him a mighty pile upon the ground, all hung with helms, and war-shields, and bright byrnies, even as he had entreated them; and in the midst of it the sorrowing men laid their great king, their belovèd lord. Then the warriors kindled the greatest of funeral fires upon the mound. Uprose the wood-

smoke, black above the flame; blazing fire roared
(mingled with a sound of weeping when the
tumult of the wind was stilled), until, hot within
the breast, it had consumed the bony frame.   Sad
at heart, with care-laden soul, they mourned the
fall of their lord.   Likewise the aged wife,[1] with
hair upbound, sorrowing in heart, sang a dirge
for Beowulf; oft said she dreaded sore that evil
days would come upon her, and much bloodshed,
fear of the warrior, and shame and bondage.—
Heaven swallowed up the smoke.

Then the Weder people made a mound upon
the cliff—it was high and broad, to be seen afar
of seafaring men; and ten days they built it, the
war-hero's beacon.   They made a wall round
about the ashes of the fire, even as the wisest of
men could most worthily devise it there.   Within
the mound they put the rings and the jewels, all
the adornments which the brave-hearted men had
taken from the hoard; they let the earth hold the
treasure of heroes, put the gold in the ground,
where it still remains, as useless unto men as it
was of yore.

Then warriors, sons of princes, twelve in all,

---

[1] Bugge's reconstruction of another mutilated passage
(five lines) is used.   Nothing else is known of the " wife."

rode about the mound; they were minded to bewail their sorrow, mourn their king, utter the dirge, and speak of their hero; they praised his courage and greatly commended his mighty deeds. Thus it is fitting that a man should praise his lord in words and cherish him in heart when he must forth from the fleeting body.

So the Geatish people, companions of his hearth, mourned the fall of their lord; said that he was a mighty king, the mildest and kindest of men, most gracious to his people, and most desirous of praise.[1]

[1] Cf. Tennyson's *Guinivere*, ll. 478–80.

INDEX OF PROPER NAMES

The approximate pronunciation is indicated is parentheses

Ælfhere (Alf'herra), see Wiglaf.

Æschere (Ash'herra), Hrothgar's councillor, slain by Grendel's mother.

Beanstan (Bay'an-stan), father of Breca.

Beowulf (Bay'o-wolf), the Dane, an ancestor of Hrothgar, not the hero of the poem.

Beowulf the Geat, hero of the poem, son of Ecgtheow, and by his mother nephew to Hygelac.

Breca (Brekka), a chief of the Brondings who contended with Beowulf in swimming.

Brondings, see Breca.

Dæghrefn (Dag'hraven), "Day Raven," a warrior of the Hugs, slain by Beowulf.

Danes, variously called Scyldings, Ingwines, Hrethmen, North-, South-, East-, and West-Danes. The people of Hrothgar, whose home is apparently in southern Sweden.

Eadgils (Ay'ad gils), son of Ohthere, who with his brother, Eandmund, is banished from Sweden because of rebellion; they flee to the land of the Geats, where Heardred is king. An invasion of the Geatish land follows, headed by Onela, king of the Swedes. King Heardred is slain, and Onela leaves Beowulf to succeed to the throne. Beowulf later aids Eadgils in avenging himself.

Eanmund (Ay'an mund), brother to Eadgils· slain by Weohstan.

Ecglaf (Edge'laf), father of Unferth.

Ecgtheow (Edge'theow), father of Beowulf, and husband to the only daughter of King Hrethel.

Ecgwela (Edge'wella), an ancestor of the Danes.

Elan (Ay'lan), ? daughter of Healfdene, and sister of Hrothgar.

Eofor (Ay'o vor), a Geatish warrior, brother of Wulf, who fought with the Swedish King Ongentheow.

Eomær (Ay' o mare), son of Offa and Thrytho.

Eormanric (Ay'or man ric), Hermanric, king of the Ostrogoths.

Eotens (Ay'o tens), the people of Finn; perhaps the Jutes.

Finn, king of the Eotens, who abducted Hildeburh, a Danish princess.

Finns, the people in whose land Beowulf finds himself after his swimming-match with Breca.

Fitela (Fit'el la), the Norse Sinfiötli, nephew to Sigemund.

Folcwalda (Folk'wall da), father of Finn.

Franks, one of the nations that defeated Hygelac in his last raid.

Freawaru (Fray'a wa roo), Hrothgar's daughter who is betrothed to Ingeld.

Frisians, one of the tribes who defeated Hygelac; also the people of Finn.

Froda, father of Ingeld.

Garmund, father of Offa.

Geats (Yay'ats, *or*, Gay'ats), variously called Hrethlings, Weders, Weder-, Sea- and War-Geats. Beowulf's people.

Gifths, ? the Gepidae.

Grendel, an evil monster, descendant of Cain.

Guthlaf (Gooth'laf), a Danish warrior who, with Oslaf, brought reinforcements in the battle against King Finn.

Hæreth (Hair'eth), father of Hygd.

Hæthcyn (Hath'kin), second son of Hrethel, king of the Geats. He kills his elder brother, Herebeald, and later succeeds to the throne, but is slain by Ongentheow.

Half-Danes, the tribe to which Hnæf belonged.

Halga, younger brother to Hrothgar.

Hama, the man who stole the Brising necklace.

Healfdene (Hay'alf den na), father of Hrothgar and king of the Danes.

Heardred (Hay'ard red), Hygelac's son, for a short time king of the Geats, under the regency of Beowulf.

Heathobards (Hay'a tho bards), the tribe to which Ingeld belongs.

Heatholaf (Hay'a tho laf), slain by Ecgtheow.

Heathoraemas (Hay'a tho ray''mas), the people among whom Breca finds himself after his swimming-match.

Helmings, the people to whom Wealtheow belongs.

Hemming, kinsman of Offa and Eomær.

Hengest, the enemy of Finn, who attempts to avenge the abduction of his sister.

Heorogar (Hay o ro gar), Hrothgar's elder brother.

Heorot (Hay o rot), Hrothgar's hall.

Heoroweard (Hay'o ro waird), son of Heorogar.

Heorobeald (Hay'o ro bay"ald), King Hrethel's son, slain by his brother.

Heremod (Herra mod), a king of the Danes, twice men-.ioned as a type of the cruel and incompetent sovereign.

Hereric (Herra rik), Heardred's uncle.

Hetwaras, one of the tribes that fought against Hygelac in his last raid.

Hildeburh (Hilda burgh), see Finn.

Hnaef (Hnaf), brother of Hengest and his assistant; see Hengest.

Hoc, father of Hildeburh.

Hondscio (Hond'she o), Beowulf's thane, slain by Grendel.

Hreosnabeorh (Hray'os na bay"orh), scene of the invasion by Onela and Ohthere.

Hrethel (Hreh'thel), Hygelac's father and Beowulf's grand-father, formerly king of the Geats.

Hrethlings, Hrethel's people, the Geats.

Hrethmen, a name of the Danes.

Hrethric, Hrothgar's eldest son.

Hrothgar, king of the Danes, builder of Heorot.

Hrothmund, Hrothgar's younger son.

Hrothulf, Hrothgar's nephew.

Hrunting (Hroon'ting), the name of Unferth's sword.

Hugs, a race allied to the Franks.

Hunlaf, a "son of Hunlaf," is mentioned as the slayer of Hengest.

Hygd (Higd), Hygelac's gracious queen.

Hygelac (Hig'el ak), Beowulf's uncle, king of the Geats.

Ingeld, betrothed to Freawaru.

Ingwine (Ing'winna), Ingaevones, a name of the Danes.

Nægling (Nag'ling), name of a sword of Beowulf's.

INDEX OF PROPER NAMES

147